TIME AFTER TIME

TIME AFTER TIME

WRITTEN & ILLUSTRATED BY

CHRISTOPHER HARVILL

To my mom, who heard my first Avery Black

story 40-years ago.

Pleased To Meet You

I AM ASKED WHAT I AM.

THERE IS A SIMPLE CHILD'S GAME CALLED *TELEPHONE*.

Whisper something to your neighbor. Pass it on around a circle. Watch what was said now changed at the end. Stretch the game over millennia, and you have legends. Folklore. Myths. Fairy Tales.

I am that.

I whispered at the Beginning, and I will be listening at the End.

MY DOOR OPENED TO LOS ANGELES, MARCH 15, 2020.
I WAS ALREADY TOO LATE.

Down an alleyway, a man walked casually with Eve lumped over his broad shoulders. He wore a tailored suit and black shoes so polished they seemed to be made of obsidian. It is a stark contrast to the low-income apartments on either side that mask me in their shadows. The smells there were wrong. Instead of the odor of trash and stagnant sewers, there came a breath of sulfur. A wisp of…brimstone?

"Put her down," I demanded.

The man continued on as though he hadn't a care in the world, as if he were carrying a briefcase after work instead of a woman. Her very existence predicated I did not let this man get away. So, I went within, preparing a sigil that would prevent him from going further. I felt its energy course through me, just as I had sensed Eve's dark unconsciousness. Thus, the door opened here. Yet, something was wrong. The power this evil held was something I had not anticipated.

"Put her down!"

I said it again in a commanding tone that echoed off the concrete buildings. The man halted beneath a streetlamp. Its halo sizzled, then flickered to black.

"I heard you the first time, little paladin." The man's deep but hollow voice sounded from the darkness. "Did you feel the crack in the dam?"

He shifted, adjusting his grip on Eve. Her body jostled then wilted back to immobility, appearing as if no soul molded its form any longer. The man glanced over his shoulder at me; his eyes glinted in the light of my power. Within them, I found everything I needed to know.

Back foot braced, I lifted my right hand in protection; my left was aglow with the Norse symbol of strength. Then, an all-encompassing gale froze the surrounding air. I could feel its bone chill as the pavement on which I stood cracked. A sudden blinding flash followed, and it seemed as if the world had detonated on its axis. I was knocked to the ground.

Perhaps it was the drone of an engine approaching that saved me from another final assault. More likely, The Elder simply wished to make a statement. A parting gift so profound that birds for miles took flight, and dogs moaned across the city in a pitiful song of fear. Yet, even after it was gone, I remained on my knees, trounced beneath its cataclysmic power.

Rowdy hockey stopped his 1941 *Indian* motorcycle at the mouth of the alley, the glare of its headlamp washing over me. I knew he would find me; his kind excelled in such things. He looked around for threats, and seeing none, helped me to my feet.

"What was that awful noise?"

He asked the question with a twinge of excitement. Had I said vampires, he would have said, "Great! Let's go kick their ass!"

I took in a deep breath. "Laughter. It was laughing at me – knew I was coming."

I adjusted my Windsor glasses, leveling my gaze on the scout as he took off his Dodger cap and ran his fingers through his long brown hair. Then, he put it on again and looked back at me. Rowdy was always ready. Beneath the leather jacket and white t-shirt he wore, he had a sinewy form that seemed ever tense and poised to strike.

"Get Jo and Silver. Comb the city for Eve. It will whisper in her ear – Knowledge will seep, then spill. We have to wake her before it's too late."

"Too late for what?" Rowdy asked.

Los Angeles was about to explode.

KNOWLEDGE IS POWER.

TRUE KNOWLEDGE IS UNSTAINED BY A PERSON'S OPINION OR in the telling. That was Eve. That was why Los Angeles had started to rip itself apart. Police sirens wailed toward the explosion at One Police Plaza. Downtown street gangs from The Dulows to White Fence, whose violence was kept tenuously in check by their self-proclaimed boundaries, had gone to war.

Rowdy, Jo, and Silver scoured the city from atop their motorbikes. No sign of Eve. From Celtic to Incan, I had used every sigil of finding. Still, nothing. So, I went with the only clue I had. As the door opened, a chime rang above me. Cassandra entered the room through a beaded curtain. Her hair went from deep black in the shadows to red within the lamplight. She wore a floor-length green dress that rippled as she walked like tall grass in the breeze. Her loveliness engulfed the room; impossible to drink in as she oiled her way toward me, hips swaying.

"*The Ides of March.* The date didn't elude me. How are you mixed up with this?" I inquired. "I wish it would be Baba or Le Fay. I need straight answers."

Cassandra sighed. "I'm fine, thank you for asking. No Baba. Russian hurts my throat. As for Le Fay?" She came within an inch of me and placed a finger to my lips. "Be careful what you wish for."

For a long moment, she scrutinized me. Beneath her regard, I dared not squirm.

"We liked the old you," she remarked casually. "With the lance. We've missed your…musk."

"What do you get from this?" I asked.

She laughed coyly. "A partnership. Call it melancholy. Ennui. So, we rang you."

Witches. As. Partners. At the thought of it, I turned away from her.

"Rome is burning outside, Avery," Cassandra said. "That's your name now? Such Power in names. But your scouts can't find what's beneath their very noses?"

The innuendoes were her way around the curse that stemmed from a millennium of not being truly understood. Cassandra, the daughter of the last king of Troy, had been a gifted but tormented prophetess. Yet, she seemed assuaged by the passing of time, and vestiges of truth still laced her statements; the lilt of Greek in her voice was nearly irresistible.

"Sigils and signs fail you. Can't find what's in plain sight?" she asked.

I turned back to her, and she pressed against me. I inhaled the perfume of her skin – mint, marjoram, and cypress, the aromas of her birthplace. She slipped her hand beneath my coat and caressed the flowing ink on my chest.

"We will make a great team, Illustrated Man."

Her voice accented her beauty like a string of pearls might highlight a neckline. It seemed to sing off her tongue, her Grecian ancestry lending it an ancient air. She studied me, searching for something in my eyes. Then, her brow furrowed, surprised by something she saw as she looked at her reflection in my glasses.

"What do you think of curses?" she whispered.

I took a moment to formulate my answer. A woman such as Cassandra, cursed for spurning the advances of the god Apollo, had her own biased perspective on the matter. I wondered why she asked me the question in the first place. Why would she be interested in my point of view?

"Everyone and everything is cursed, Cassandra." We held each other's gaze, standing so close it was as if the next words I spoke held some unknown weight to our future. "The hawk has talons but never the song of the sparrow. It's never about the curse. It's about whether we let that curse define us."

"How does yours define you, Avery Black?" she asked.

I reached behind me and took The Doorway's knob in my hand. I gave it a slight turn and felt its weight. Its significance, perhaps.

"With every knock, Cassandra. With every knock."

"Go then. Smite. Like Eve, you should taste the fruit of your labor."

Cassandra put her hand atop mine and pushed the door open.

"Oh, one last thing." Cassandra kissed me, her tongue running across my lips just as she pulled away. "Nothing can beat this Elder."

A smile from her, and I walked through the door. The sounds of chaos and catastrophe blared. Police lights flashed red and blue through a curtain of smoke. Then, the door shut behind me.

Time to solve the riddle. Time to earn my keep.

I ASK.

THE SYMBOLS, SIGILS, AND SIGNS EMBEDDED IN MY SKIN have spanned generations and traversed millenniums. Each possessed ancient alchemy that required me to request their use and ethereal force as a sign of respect. I understood this, and I believed I would be asking a lot of them today.

I Ask for communication. Rowdy answered my call; his voice was clear in my mind. I told him of my meeting with Cassandra and what I discerned from her cryptic euphemisms.

"Under our noses, huh? Think Eve is in the sewers?" Rowdy paused, thinking. "Lotta tunnels down there, Av."

"The violence started Downtown. *'Can't find what's in plain sight,'* Cassandra said. *"Fruits of her labor."* Another clue. "Rowdy, Los Angeles won't survive if you don't wake Eve. Nothing will."

I severed the line. *'Power in names.* It led me here – Powers Tower. Its windowed façade resembled wings wrapping around a central coil. Not very subtle. Nevertheless, why would an Elder run for mayor?

I entered the lobby, and the receptionist motioned toward the elevator.

"Top Floor. You're expected Mr. Black."

The elevator doors opened on a giant suite. No furniture. Polished wooden floors and thirty-foot high ceilings. The man from the alley stood before the office's windows. His attention was focused on the city beyond the glass.

"Do you like what I've done to this place?" He motioned to Los Angeles and the fires that painted the horizon red. "In Xanadu did Kubla Khan a stately pleasure dome decree!"

Coleridge's poem. Every little clue helped.

"What do you want with Eve?" I asked, getting to the point.

He turned to face me and smiled. It might have been a sneer, but it was hard to tell past his manicured goatee and overtly obnoxious sense of self-importance.

"I took the girl for them, and you came," the man said.

He spoke with an English accent, which hinted at his origin. Perhaps he masked it with an All-American tone when speaking to the masses. He might have even added a Texas twang to it – worked for the Bush family.

I bowed but never took my eyes from his.

"Elder, I have come here as a courtesy. Give me Eve."

"You make demands," he began. "As a courtesy? Eve is theirs. They put her to sleep – shook the tree. Now, the city burns. It's what they promised if I didn't end you."

He circled me, blowing an inhuman plume of steam from his nostrils. A talon protruded from his shoe and dragged a gash along the floor.

"My name marks this place now. I will be elected their king."

Dragons. They loved to talk.

"The human voters give me their names." His voice strained, too large for his throat. "So mannnny names. Birthplaces. Making me stronger. Backing me. Defending me. Working for me. All just a beginning…"

Laughter exploded from his mouth as the skin along its side tore from his face. Sword-length fangs swelled from his bleeding gums, and his human mask fell in clumps onto the floor. The beast shed its façade, making a grand entrance into the room – always grand entrances with these kind.

"What is their emperor called? President? I will grind this time to dust. Nothing. Will. Stop. Me."

Another blast from his nostrils fogged the glass wall to my back.

"Who is manipulating you? An Elder? You're being played," I baited him. "It's called The Long Con. It's me they want!"

The eldritch blue flame from his half dragon-half man mouth blew me through the glass. I fell, shards of glass coming down around me like sharpened rain. Still, I only hoped for one thing, that Rowdy had gotten to a produce stand in time.

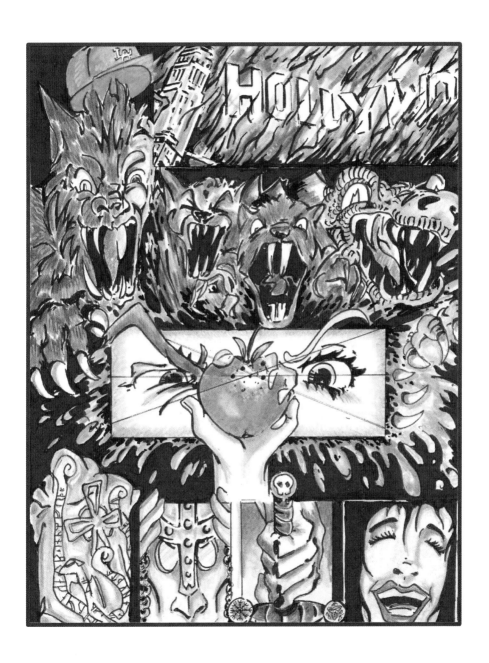

MY NAME IS RICHIE CROWE, BUT EVERYONE CALLS ME ROWDY.

I AM TWENTY-TWO YEARS OLD FOREVER, OR AT LEAST UNTIL my curse is lifted. I can change into an eight-foot-tall lychan. I like the Dodgers. Big pancake fan.

Now, I stood with Jo looking down into the sewer. The stench of thousands of gallons of raw sewage wafted up in our faces.

"What a delightful fragrance," she said.

"I've smelled worse," I quipped.

Jo gave me a dubious look. "Really? When?"

I shrugged. "Alright, I'll admit it's not so delightful, but with about hundred scented candles, we can make this place work."

Jo shook her head. Her hair was matted down with sweat from her motorcycle helmet. She looked stunning.

"So, this is 'Eve' Eve?" she asked. "Like Adam and Eve?"

"So, Avery says. Tree of Knowledge. Rib of Adam." I shone the flashlight into the sewer but could not see anything.

The murk was doing its job. "The snake whispered evil thoughts into Eve's ear. So now, if you whisper in her ear, she will release evil thoughts. Gangs in L.A. started fighting. Hollywood sign is toast. Tear gas at City Hall. Now, we gotta stop the negative flow."

Jo stared at me skeptically. "Or?"

"Chaos. Piña Coladas – getting caught in the rain – making love at midnight. Gone. So, pressure's on."

Silver roared in on his bike, jumping off and letting his ride hit the curb at speed, cartwheel over the sidewalk, and smash into the brick wall beyond. Silver was a man of few words but big on an entrance. He walked up and tossed me his satchel.

"Found a 7-11 on Olive and 8th," he said, then glanced down into the open sewer hole. "And I think I heard Avery falling from a building earlier. I hope he's alright."

"Hope is Avery's stock in trade. He falls out of buildings for attention," I replied.

"They hid Eve under the Central Library," Silver said, his expression admiring the idea. "Lotta book smarts here. Easy to hide someone from The Tree of Knowledge."

He cracked his neck, getting ready for a fight. It sounded like he had broken a baseball bat over his knee.

"It's why Avery couldn't find her," Silver continued. "And the sewer smell is why we couldn't find her either. Tailor-made for us to fail."

"So, it's a trap? For us? And it's not even Christmas," I said.

"Ugh! But the smell!" Jo complained. "If we go down there, we'll never wash the stink out of our fur."

SALVATION IN A SATCHEL –

I leaped into the darkness, changing as I fell and itching for a fight. Jo and Silver followed suit, their humanity vanishing as they called forth their lychan blood to transform them. We hit the ground standing, three of the most dangerous beasts in the world; a wrecking crew of carnage, waiting to strike.

The sound came first – a rush of snarling and squealing rage. Then, an avalanche of rats and roaches descended on us. Jo, Silver, and I formed into a tight arc and faced the onslaught with a roar of defiance. A howl of lychan rage that told the oncoming enemy that what they were in for was blood.

Battles are seldom pretty, and this one lived up to the billing as a frenzy of alligators bit and tore at us on the command of a master we could not hear. Snakes drove their fangs deep into our fur, testing our werewolf healing factors; insects stung and bit. Every living thing that made this place home came at us all at once; a suicide mission to us from Eve, who lay unconscious on a ledge at the tunnel's end. In this stew of violence, she looked to be a thousand miles away. I drove forward – slashing and ripping at the wall of creatures in my way while torrents of sewage water fouled the air. My instinct was to flee, but I had to get to Eve.

This morass of insects and animals was bad – really bad, but Avery and I had seen worse. I could endure because I had to prevail. Stakes were high; if we lost this battle, everyone would be defeated. It was like moving through quicksand. The trash-filled water pulled at my legs, caked my fur. Jo and Silver ripped and clawed a path for me, their healing factor closing their wounds as soon as they opened. Finally, I grabbed the rotted piping along the ceiling and made my way over the snakes and rats. As soon as Eve was in reach, I hurled my body toward her and prayed Avery was right. I sensed he was far away now, at the runestone, getting what Cassandra had told him would kill an Elder. A weapon from long ago. I could feel Casandra laughing at it all.

I landed in a heap beside Eve. Leaning close to her, I took an apple from my satchel and placed it in her hand. Then, the sewer beasts engulfed me.

IT WAS TIME TO END IT.

I WATCHED FROM THE BACK OF THE CROWD AT POWERS'
campaign rally, observing how he spun the recent events to his
advantage. He was soaked in the energy of his adoring
supporters. His quest to rule was not hollow. Just as he was
being used to reach me, I was being used to slay him. But by
whom? Why?

The violence that engulfed the city had dissipated since
Rowdy had rescued Eve from the sewer. She was The Mother
of All. She had tasted from The Tree of Knowledge. She had
been there at Mankind's beginning, if one chose to believe in
such things. Many people did and still do. They study the
Greek gods; ancient deities' names are still uttered every day,
pulled up on the Internet, or mentioned in prayers, which gave
them strength and power. Yet, Eve's very existence still
walking the Earth was something very few could know. Fewer
still could comprehend that a whisper into her ear could be
used to manipulate history.

A roar of applause brought my attention back to the stage.
I advanced. My skin hummed with each step, the signs upon it
beginning to sing. Prepare. Long strides took me through the

crowd, my coat snapping in my wake. Against a dragon, it was best to make an entrance.

"Son of Fafnir."

The sound of my voice caused Powers to turn his attention away from the microphones to me. I had confronted him in his tower, goading him into showing his true color; green.

"Tell me who brought you here," I beckoned. "Let me take you home, not end you. As an Elder, you deserve…"

He tilted his head back to laugh, but the sound was swallowed in his throat. I lifted the Celtic symbol of concealment. The sword in my hand glinted in the sun as I raised it. Sigurd's sword, *Nothung*, from Norse mythology, had slain this dragon's ancestors. I went to retrieve it after my sigils saved me from my fall from Powers' lair. Nothing, indeed, can kill an Elder – Cassandra and her riddles.

"You cannot beat me here," I said. "Did they tell you that?"

The Elder burst from his human disguise like a rotted rag; its dragon wingspan blocked the sun. Then, posturing, it roared and belched steam. I spun, and the Iroquois sign of protection dispersed the crowd. I was not quick enough to avoid the talon claw of the dragon that tore into the flesh of my back. I howled at the pain and pointed a fist alight with Celtic runes at my foe. The power coursing through my arm drove back my adversary. Then, a beat from the dragon's wings sent cedar leaves slashing through the air like bullets at my ethereal shield. Flames spewed past its sharpened teeth, but I raised *Nothung,* and it swallowed the heat before it reached me. Suddenly, the trees behind me ignited and were engulfed by fire. The hot winds from it whipped my hair.

"I will ram that blade through your eternal heart!" the Elder bellowed.

Then, it lashed out with its tail and wrapped it around my torso, squeezing painfully.

"Do you feel your end? Do you feel your death, little…"

I felt the vibrations first. I opened my hand, and the city of Los Angeles answered. Every sign within its boundaries shook – every symbol from every synagogue and church. Millions of icons over countless generations came to me, spoke to me, lent me their strength, for I am their avatar through time.

I was no longer on the defensive. Blade first, I charged. Imbued with the power of my sigils, I moved at great velocity and surprised the dragon. It reared backward, exposing its underbelly. I drove the sword forward and pierced the flesh through its scales. The Elder roared. Its wings flayed at me. As it fought to give itself room from *Nothung,* I could see its eyes narrow with recognition of the blade.

"Not its first time drinking the blood of a dragon," I said.

The dragon and I circled each other.

"I will fit your head on a pike as a warning to all who stand before me." The Elder threatened.

His reaction as pretty much what I expected.

Another burst of eldritch flame, but *Nothung* protected me. The Elder roared, and its wings beat in rage. Although the force of the attack flipped cars on the street and ripped trees from their roots, my sigils held before me kept him at bay.

"This does not need to end in death!" I hollered at him above the tumult.

Enraged, the beast came at me as if in answer.

I would need to gain my answers another way. Death it would be. I brought the sword down into him. In its death throes, it uttered a single word.

"Hopeless…"

It was a word meant especially for me.

WEREWOLVES OF LONDON

WE WERE BEING HUNTED.

LIKE THE FOX AT THE END OF THE CHASE, WE HAD BEEN RUN to ground on the dirty cobblestone streets of nineteenth-century London. Avery's sigils danced from his body to his fingertips as he cast every symbol of power and protection his eons of travel had given him to summon. Celtic to Navajo, Roman to Hebrew, he lit the square we were in with light. The werewolves were striking us from all sides. We were stranded at the center of their fury hurricane.

Cassandra wielded a bat of some kind with both hands, protecting our flank. In a tattered ballgown, the Grecian witch who probably apologized to grass after she walked on it was a frenzy of movement and screaming with rage. At my side was Sacajawea – Jo, the love of my life. In her lychan form, she slashed and bit. Despite her ferocity, her healing factor had reached its limit after countless attacks had spilled her blood. Mine was already depleted. Neither of us had the primordial strength left to withstand the onslaught. She looked at me, and we knew our end was a death dance in slow motion.

Suddenly crippled by the painful blow of a werewolf assault, Cassandra went down to one knee. Then, a deep slash across Jo's leg caused her to fall. Avery, desperate but still determined, cast one last shield of protection with everything he had. I howled in final defiance of our demise.

We were history.

But that's not how it all started.

PROLOGUE
THE WITCH'S CABAL

THOUGH A BRAZIER WAS LIT IN THE MIDDLE OF THE LARGE oval table, its glow and warmth barely penetrated the darkness. The women seated around it enjoyed the inky blackness. They had spent lifetimes within such gloom. A black cat, almost invisible except for its piercing yellow eyes, stalked the tabletop.

"He dispatched The Elder," a woman spoke in a feline hiss.

"He is not to be trifled with," said a voice in ancient Egyptian.

"We risk everything should we be found out by The Eternal Man."

The words seemed to crawl from its speaker's throat, gargling their way to pronouncement.

"Do you wish to live in legend and fairy tales or once more step into grandeur?" The woman stood and eyed the others at the table, defying an answer to her query. "The dragon was a message. Nothing more. Our first move in the game."

A fetid creature, her hair slimy and dank, leaned forward to challenge the statement, but the black cat hissed at her. She drew back.

"Now, now, Agatha. None of that," the standing woman cautioned.

She motioned a hand toward the feline. It came to her and rubbed its head into her palm. Yet, it never drew its mystic yellow gaze from the others seated in the gloom.

"The plan runs apace." The woman leading the Cabal glanced to the only empty chair at the table. "Cassandra will work her charms. We will twist his portal. Damarchus will dismiss of Black's paladin." She paused, then drew in an expectant breath. "Then, our turn will come."

Speaking in tongues ancient and forgotten, there was a murmuring of agreement from the gathering. Their hands, rotted and skeletal, reached toward the brazier. The fire responded; its flames leaped before them, causing their fingers to glow with powerful heat.

The woman leading The Cabal stood out because, unlike the others, her hand was supple and smooth. Her long fingers were adorned with glistening rings. The flames licked at her ruby red nails and danced in patterns along her skin like performers on a stage. Then, the fire began to take the form of a flatted rectangle of blazing yellow orange. The details sharpened to show The Doorway of Avery Black Investigation.

"Now, Avery," the woman said, her hungry smile revealing perfect white teeth. "Hope, hope, hope to the last."

She clenched her fingers into a fist.

Knock. Knock.

ROWDY'S STORY

When they made their entrance, I was seated at the bar, jacket off, Old Fashion in hand. Drinks and dancing had become a bit of a thing, and I did not want to miss it.

Avery was in a dark blue tuxedo, hair tied back. Cassandra was – well, Cassandra. Hair flowing and wearing a gown that trailed along the floor as if trying to keep up. The two instantly commanded the room. No surprise. He had been around a zillion years, and she had been the girlfriend of the chariot god. Hence, they both possessed that *je ne sais quoi* that kept every eye in the room on them. It was December 1945. The war was won.

With a nod from Benny Goodman, the band erupted into a timely melody. Avery and Cassandra moved across the dance floor as if on a cloud. Quickstep. Left whisks. Viennese variations. Feather touches to the hand, slight tilts of the shoulder, their moves were synchronized perfection. Then, Avery dipped Cassandra; their lips were a hairs-breath apart. I gave them a second, letting that building sexual tension since they had met in Los Angeles get closer to the red.

"Gimme rock and roll any day," I said, sticking my face in between them.

I nodded across the room to The Doorway, standing unseen to all but the three of us.

Avery seemed perplexed. "Odd. I usually sense its arrival."

"Distracted?" Cassandra asked coyly, touching his arm.

Maintaining our calm and style, we approached it. Then, Avery took the knob in hand. Steeling himself, he made sure we were ready before opening it. Beyond the door frame, it was night, and the chime of a big clock reverberated through the air. Then came the unmistakable smell, and I knew that it was all wrong. Instantly, I threw myself in front of Avery and Cassandra, shoving them back as I was drawn forward. Thick fur formed over my human body, my teeth and nails protruded and became deadly sharp as I transformed into a lychan. Then, the door slammed shut behind me, and I roared forcefully as if to get open again. It was a badass thing, my roar; a 'curdle milk,' 'wet your pants,' 'send you home to momma' type of thing. Twenty answered me. I had heard a pack of three howling after a hunt, but it was nothing like this.

Suddenly, they came at me, so I went at them. It was my kind of dancing. Travel with Avery long enough, and you learn a few hundred fighting moves forgotten over time. These practical techniques and ancient defensive variations helped me take out three werewolves before the first of them hit the ground. Still, the odds were not in my favor. Claws, fangs, and muscle hammered me. A brick building to my rear offered a fire escape. I took to it, hoping to get some elevation on my attackers and meet them one-on-one.

THE BLOW CAME WITHOUT WARNING.

A STRIKE FROM BEHIND THAT FELT LIKE A SLEDGEHAMMER. Another swing from a weighted staff sent me spiraling back down to earth. I hit the cobblestone street hard, and my attacker was already on me. Grabbing my scalp, he drove me muzzle first into the muck that filled the alley. Once. Twice. A third time. He was crazy strong.

"Well, boyo, you didn't disappoint," he said, catching his breath.

He had an English accent. *Ugh.*

"Those blows would have ripped a normal man's head clean off." He cracked his back. It sounded like a two-by-four being broken in half. "But we aren't normal, are we, pal?" He pressed me down. "Introductions. I'm Damarchus Hill. We've been waiting."

I could hear the gloating. I spat out blood. Then, I gritted my teeth to show as much spunk as a guy whose ass was just handed to him could.

"Gonna have to settle for me, buddy." I tried to turn, but he held my head fast. "Avery won't fall for a trap like that. Not in a million years."

The pack howled, but the Damarchus guy actually laughed. So much for spunk.

"Not to worry. We'll get around to your Doorway Man soon enough, Mr. Crowe. But you see…" he leaned in close and drove the point of his cane hard into my neck. "This trap was set for you."

THE DOOR WOULD NOT OPEN.

I HAD TRAVELED TIME AND THE WORLD, BUT NEVER HAD THE knob denied me. Yet, now as many times as I tried, it was as though it was locked from the other side. In the dance hall, people in tuxedos and dresses had backed away from Cassandra and me into a rough semi-circle, gawking at the couple who had disappeared then materialized again from thin air.

Irritated, I called on the Navajo sigil of unseeing, and Cassandra and I faded from their view, becoming invisible and silent to their senses. It worked very well for the Native Americans in their hunting and trapping for the centuries before the European incursions. It served the same for the two of us while I tried to decipher this conundrum before me.

"Don't you have the key?" Cassandra asked and looked through the keyhole. "I can't see anything."

"Because there is nothing there," I replied.

I had considered, up to this moment, The Doorway as a kind of partner. However, now was at odds with me. It had blocked my request and intention to get back to Rowdy, almost mocking me in its silence.

"The door answers when I ask. Knocks when it needs me to answer."

"Did you ask nicely, Avery?" Cassandra eyed me. "I have found in the past weeks you can, at times, be a tad caustic."

I did not feel that merited a response.

Cassandra looked squarely at the wooden door, shoulders back, addressing it.

"Can we please go help our friend? He may be in trouble," she said.

She tried the knob herself. It failed to turn. I delicately took her hand from the door, and she saw the concern on my face.

"Avery, I can tell by your expression this has never happened before."

I turned her squarely to me.

"I believe I know *where* Rowdy is, but I will need help in the *when*. Have you had a vision or premonition? Anything that will lead me to him?"

She shook her head. "It doesn't work that way. I'm sorry. What I feel rarely reveals itself in black in white."

"Then we'll need help finding him once we're there," I replied.

People had begun to move forward. Several had started to reach out into the space ahead of them, as if sensing something there they could not quite see. The sigil's power would bleed away should someone lay hands on us. I mentally asked The Door, as I had for times beyond measure, for it to take me away. Still, nothing happened. Then, I felt Cassandra touch my arm as people closed in from the dance floor.

"But what if it doesn't answer?" she asked.

"That is an excellent question," I responded.

I took hold of the doorknob and turned it.

THE DOOR OPENED.

THE SCENT OF PINE AND SPRUCE WAS CARRIED ON A GENTLE
breeze We had left the dance hall of the twentieth century for
a Montana forest in the nineteenth. Two seconds later, a bone
knife hit the Ponderosa pine tree just inches from my face and
sank deep into its trunk. I looked in the direction it had come
from and saw Sacajawea emerge from the forest shadows. She
was a beauty of a woman in her early twenties with sun-
browned skin that melded seamlessly with the surrounding
wilderness. After her travels with Lewis and Clark, she had
been bitten by a werewolf while in Boston. Her transformation
had forced her to leave her children to keep them safe. She fled
to the world of trees and rivers that she knew so well. Rowdy
found her there and showed her how to live with what she had
become. It had forged a bond between them, a kind of
synchronicity, even when far apart and worlds away.

"Good to see you're doing well, Jo," I said.

"Rowdy is late. He's never late," she replied, troubled.

She spoke in the Siouan tongue of the tribe that kidnapped
her as a young girl. I used a sigil of understanding. Its mark

illuminated for an instant on my skin. We could now all understand each other. Language-wise, at least.

Cassandra glared at the knife in the tree, then back at Jo.

"You could have killed him!"

"He should be more vigilant. He is seldom not unless…distracted." Jo studied Cassandra. Then, she lifted her nose to the wind as if to catch a scent. "She reeks of evil, Black."

"She is a sister of Skadegamutc," I said. "But she is not evil."

"So, you say." Jo went and yanked the knife from the pine, never taking her eyes off Cassandra. "Where is my mate?"

"Rowdy is lost in time," I replied. "We'll need you to find him once we are close."

"And the witch?" Sacajawea asked. Eyes narrowing, she tested the weight of her knife.

"You want to throw your knife at *me* now?" Cassandra said accusingly. "What have I done to you? I was dancing just a few moments ago!"

"I know what your type is like, creature."

Cassandra advanced on Jo. "As Rowdy would say, you do not know Jack!"

I put a hand on Jo's throwing arm before she could raise it. Witches. Werewolves. No one said this would be easy.

Cassandra gestured to the door. "How can we even get to Rowdy if that will not take us?"

I picked up a branch, stripping it of leaves. It would be suitable.

"We use the back door."

THE SUN WAS SETTING WHEN I OPENED THE DOOR ONTO WILTSHIRE, SOUTHERN ENGLAND.

THE DAY'S FINAL BEAM OF LIGHT PASSED THROUGH Stonehenge's gray monoliths. The sarsen blocks still watched over a plain of green grass as they had since the day they were set into place. I saw the uncomfortable looks on Jo and Cassandra's faces as they took in the five-thousand-year-old site.

"I imagine you're feeling the dead. It was a burial site once upon a day."

"This will take us to Rowdy?" Jo asked warily, knife raised.

"It's also a lunar calendar." Branch in hand, I started up the slight rise of a hill. "If you know how to use it."

"And you do?" Cassandra seemed skeptical, following me into the rock alignments.

"I was here when they built it," I said.

"Who is 'they'?" Jo asked.

"That would be telling," I replied, adjusting my glasses.

I followed what is now known as the Aubrey Holes, counting as I went.

Cassandra grabbed at my jacket. "We still don't know where to go."

"I heard Big Ben sound just as Rowdy pushed us back through the door. So, London. You said Black *in* White, rather than *and*. I believe that refers to me and Whitechapel, a district in London's East End, which is within ear shot of the great clock."

I held the branch over a small indentation in the grass and eyed our placement within the horseshoe of rock around us.

"August 8th, 1888. The strongest full moon during his spree." I smiled at Cassandra. "I believe I do know Jack."

I plunged the stick down, and we were there. In the room. With the body. At that precise moment, Jack the Ripper turned to us with a blade in hand.

I SAT BACK AND WAITED.

I WAS IN A DARK STONE BASEMENT, CLIMBING THE WALLS. literally. When you are a werewolf/lychan like me, the pacing does not cut it. Since they had tossed me down there, I had stayed in my human form. It made it easier on the senses, especially because I smelled like a guy who had just lost a fight with a sewage pipe.

Where the hell was Avery? I had shoved him out of the doorway as soon as I smelled the werewolves in the alley, but I figured he would be back in a second, sigils blazing. I know him; he would not have just returned to the dance floor with Cassy, even if she was the most beautiful woman in history. But me Avery had history, too. He would be coming for me any minute.

"He's not coming for you." Damarchus Hill's pompous English accent rang out from the top of the stairway. "They took care of that for me – so you and I can have some time to ourselves."

He came down the steps slowly, twirling a weighted red ball cane.

"You're not my type. I fall for the cackling Joker-style villain," I said with hubris. "You cackle? Bet you do. When you're all by yourself trying on straight jackets. C'mon, tell me how you're gonna conquer the world. Make it a good one."

"With your help," he said bluntly.

That *was* a good one.

"You really are magnificent. Everything they promised." Damarchus looked at his staff; the red ball had a peculiar inner glow. "Imagine what we could do together."

"Make fondue?" I asked sarcastically.

Damarchus reached the bottom step.

"We had to wait until you awoke – didn't want to risk anything. When I knocked you out, you reverted to your human state." He said that with a bit of repulsion, then his eyes gleamed. "Instantly. Amazing."

Oh, I was going to give him amazing any second now. Magnificent, too. Toss in some astonishing, flabbergasting, and incredible just for good measure.

"He calls himself Avery Black now?" Damarchus asked, testing the name on his tongue. "A very black what, do you imagine? Has he told you about me? We were…roommates." He laughed at the word. "I would have been glad to end him, but they wanted him for themselves."

"They? So, you're a puppet. This is my surprised face." I yawned, whirling my finger in a circular motion so that he would get on with it. "You were on a conquer the world rant."

"They told me that he and The Doorway have been quite irritating. Showing up at the most..." Damarchus searched for the word. "Inconvenient of times."

This guy really liked to hear himself talk, but I had heard enough. I changed to lychan and planted my fist square into his chest, blowing him backward a good ten feet. Then, I tossed him up the stairway with enough force to shatter the steps as he flew through them. The whole thing took about three seconds.

"How's that for irritating?"

He pushed himself back on the stairs as I advanced. We reached a hallway in an industrial building with glass walls. It smelled of oil and machinery.

"You don't understand," he said, his accent losing its bravado. "They hunt us! When the moon is full, they hunt us like game! The opportunity I'm giving you. The opportunity you're giving US!"

"Oh, I understand." In lychan form, my voice takes on a gravelly quality. It makes for good theatre. "You thought you were going to get an 'A' in World Conquering Class. But I'm afraid you're about to flunk the final."

I grabbed him by the neck and chucked his ass out the window behind him. He fell onto the fire escape and looked up at me. Snarling a bit himself, he kept the head of his staff between us as I came through the shattered glass to stand over him. I could see that he was trying to change to a werewolf. The sun was just starting to set. It was doable before the full moon rose but incredibly painful and impossible to hold. The lychan in me allowed me to change at will, day or night, full moon or not.

"They told me you wouldn't listen," he said through gritted teeth. He had his left side transformed, but that was not going to be enough.

"They?" I was at my full eight feet, looming like a giant on the metal platform. "Let's talk 'they' a bit before this ass-kicking lesson comes to an end. 'They' who? 'They' want what?

"Here. Let me show you," Damarchus replied.

He swung his cane at me. I easily pushed it aside but left myself open for a strike with the sharp nails of his left hand. He slashed my chest, causing me to bleed. I moved in, and he ripped his talon across my face. He raised his claw to show me the blood. Then, laughing, he licked it.

"How was that for a cackle, boy?" he mocked.

I am such an idiot. Damachus suddenly became full lychan, my blood mixing with his werewolf blood. I went at him full-force, but he jumped three stories to the alleyway below with lupine grace.

"Cheerio. Conquering to do," Damarchus said, and tipped his staff to his forehead in a gesture of farewell.

I came down in a heartbeat, tracking him as he ducked into a building. I had his scent. He could run. Hide. Cower. Still, I would not lose him. Mr. Werewolf with his cane might think he was dealing with a common werewolf, but I was more than that! I had lost my Dodger cap when I arrived in merry ol' England; I intended to revenge that slight in spades.

I kicked open the door he had gone through and was immediately assaulted with the overpowering odors of alcohol and ammonia. He had run into a laundry warehouse. The grinding of the machinery was deafening and unexpected. The smells were overwhelming. I staggered back out into the open and regained my bearings. Then, I gnashed my teeth in anger, knowing how neatly I had been suckered. He had gotten me to transform out of human form and let me play cat and mouse with him until he could change just enough to draw my blood. His use of the laundry building as an escape route had bought him time, but his scent was still there. It would take me a moment to find his path – might as well have been a lifetime. The moon was rising fast. From where I stood, it looked huge – a Hunter's Moon.

A hand touched my shoulder. I somehow knew it was her. Turning around, I saw Jo standing there with a concerned expression. Her face was marked with war paint. One long streak of orange with four red talon claws. Never had I seen a prettier sight. I morphed back into a human and took her hand. Our fingers intertwined as the full moon rose higher in the night sky. Avery and Cassandra stepped up behind her, and I threw my hands up in frustration.

"Well, it's about time! You make a pitstop in Hawaii? Catch some waves? Jeez, man, I'm fighting for my life here, thank you very much!"

Avery put a hand on my shoulder. "The door would not open. It took time to back here."

"You can thank me and my roundabout way of speaking for that," chimed in Cassandra.

I took my shirt off, grabbing a fresh one off the wire lines hanging outside the laundry. My other was shredded and bloody. There was no need to draw any more attention to a group that included an Indian scout, a Greek witch, and a six-foot-five time traveler with glasses that never fell off.

Jo spoke to me in her native language. She made hand gestures to tell me their story.

"You guys threw Jack the Ripper out a window?" I asked, honestly impressed. "*I* want to throw Jack the Ripper through a window!"

"Actually, he jumped out of the window," Cassandra said. "Then, he disappeared into the backstreets. Avery felt there would be time to catch him after we found you. We all felt –" Cassandra nodded toward Jo. "That you might be in danger."

"And Avery found you so you could track me," I said, taking Jo's face in my hands. "You could find anything."

I put on a cavalier expression as if the last day or so had been nothing but a trifle. A trifle, that was what they say here in England, right?

"A guy named Damarchus attacked me," I said.

Avery's face went pale, which was a lot considering the guy had a whiteboard complexion.

"You know him?" I asked. "He said you had a history, but I figured he was just blowing wind up my –"

"Damarchus Hill is one of the first werewolves," Avery interrupted. "Over a thousand years old. Maybe two. He is anger personified."

Avery surveyed the city around him with its buildings and its people going about their evening rituals. Then, he looked up at the moon.

"The city is in great peril," he said, after a moment.

A howl rose from the streets beyond. Its power shattered windows and set people to locking their doors. The echo lasted for what seemed forever. A warning. A threat. A promise, all in a single shriek of body, spirit, and blood. Avery looked at me as if he could decipher the words within it.

"The howl was Damarchus," he said.

I felt ashamed and guilty.

"He tasted my blood," I admitted hesitantly.

Absolute shock crossed Avery's face. Cassandra noticed.

"What can we do?" she asked.

Avery looked at us all.

"Run," he said.

SO, WE RAN.

DOWN JORDYN AND KAYE STREETS, OUR FEET ECHOING OFF
the cobblestones. I took the lead. Cassandra was beside me.
Rowdy and Jo were holding our flanks. With no rear guard, our
only strength was speed. Howling consumed the world around
us. The moon had become impossibly large. It now looked like
a blood moon, having been turned reddish by smoke and soot
belched out from London's countless factories and residences.

"In case you haven't noticed, we're getting our ass kicked
here!" Rowdy yelled out, shoving away a Bobbie who had been
changed as he – it, emerged from a side street.

Jo dispatched a transformed mother and child together, the
claws of the young lychan swiping up at her from its baby
carriage. I looked to Cassandra as she discarded her high heels
and tore herself away from a lychan newspaper boy pulling at
her dress.

"When you're backed against the wall, one finds how
strong they are."

One needs to read into her words to find the prophecy. I steered us toward the docks.

"Find an alley! Put the Thames to our back," I called out.

I knew the back streets of London very well from the time I had spent there with a fellow investigator. We needed a place as narrow and defensible as the mountain pass of ancient Thermopylae. It would buy us time – precious little, but time nonetheless.

Damarchus had set this trap to get Rowdy's mixed-breed blood. Now that it was done, he would bite, rip, and turn every person in London to get to me.

"Avery Black!"

The voice boomed from high above. We all stopped and looked around for its source. There, hanging from the clock arm of Big Ben, was Damarchus Hill. Like some crazed Harold Lloyd, he swung his staff and howled. His growing army of fledging lychans answered him. The sound was deafening and primal.

"We have to kill him, Avery!" Rowdy yelled at me over the din. "His bite. Their master. Kill him, and they all go!"

Rowdy cleared a channel for us through the bloodthirsty creatures just as I watched Damarchus fling himself from the clock. He moved down its face at astounding speed. Finally, we made it to the last corner and onto Brittany Square, reaching the dock just as Damarchus landed at its far end. He was massive, a dozen feet tall; his werewolf form was a tensed coil of steel cable.

"Party crasher," he snarled at me. Then, his lips pulled back in a hideous sneer. "More, the merrier."

His horde packed around him as we circled each other. I needed to get our backs to the water and use the buildings to funnel the impending attack. It would leave a last-ditch escape route. If Damarchus' lychan horde came at us from all directions, we were finished.

"Anger always came easy to you, Damarchus," I said to him.

"Get some therapy," Rowdy added. "Don't keep all that rage cooped up inside."

"My nature," Damarchus said. He struck the ground with the ball of his staff, and lightning energy swam between the pavement cracks. Sparks lit the night like a match against flint. "Hunted turned hunter."

He looked up at the moon, then at his wolves.

"No longer beholden to that damnable orb." Damarchus met my eye then gave Rowdy a nod. "Thanks to your boy there."

Rowdy charged before I could stop him, driving into Damarchus. Although trained in fighting techniques and possessing superhuman speed and strength, he was not an ancient force of nature like his adversary. The fight that ensued was savage. Despite Rowdy's tenacity, it ended with Damarchus throwing him, barely alive, at my feet like a bag of old laundry. Jo gathered him in her arms. Rowdy looked up at me in pain.

"Softened him up for you, Av," he said.

My sigils were moving on my skin. Preparing.

"Whoever put you up to this..."

"Bugger that lot," Damarchus barked. "Let's dance, Black."

"It does not have to end like this, Damarchus," I countered.

"Always the hopeful one. This ends with my boot on your neck."

Damarchus struck the ground with the staff again. More energy shot along the brick.

"I'm going to skin you a piece at a time until you give me the key to that Doorway of yours, old friend," he said, mocking. "London is just the beginning."

He motioned with his staff, glowing white-hot with his anger, to his creations.

"Rip them apart, my pets!"

They charged in a wave of hate, and my sigils glowed as I met their challenge.

IT WAS SURE TO BE OUR LAST STAND.

INSIDE THE REFUGE OF A BUILDING, WE CAUGHT OUR BREATH. Rowdy lay on the dirty floor, bleeding from countless slashes and bites along his arms and upper torso. Though some had already closed due to his remarkable healing ability, he had lost a lot of blood. Jo held him in her arms. Her own body was ravaged, and the fur covering it was matted with gore and sweat.

Cassandra was beside me, gulping air. Her red hair lay flat against her forehead, and her green gown was little more than a rag now, clinging to her soaked body like paper mache. Her eyes were wide; she had never confronted anything like this in her ancient Greek background. She had a bloodied bat in her hand. She must have picked it up to fend off our attackers. Exhausted, she slowly sat down. I had to remind myself that she was alive and not seriously injured was a miracle in and of itself.

I stood over them; the sigils of protection I was using for our barrier glowed on my hands. Other signs and symbols moved up my torso to my chest, supporting the original wards

I had cast to buy us the breathing room we now all shared. My body. My history. My mission. All were personified by the marks I carried on my skin and summoned to my cause. I could feel them, sensing the danger, gathering in a united strength like a pack of animals. Yet, I instinctively knew it would not be enough.

"Any ideas?" Rowdy asked, looking up at me.

I nodded.

"Good," Rowdy said. "Because for a minute there, I was worried that we might be in trouble in a Butch Cassidy and the Sundance Kid, last shootout kind of way."

I turned to Cassandra. I got down on one knee to look at her. She raised her bat in surprise, seeing me in a fog of shock. Touching my hand to her wrist, I used the Navajo Bird sigil, their symbol of peace, to calm her. Her vision settled. Her body relaxed.

"Such evil," she whispered.

She saw my eyes waver with pain. Then, she looked to the closed door behind me. It pulsed with a yellow glow, in sync with the symbols on my body.

"They're attempting to get through, aren't they?" she asked.

"Yes, and they will unless we take to drastic measures."

"Nuclear option," Rowdy said. "Broken Arrow."

He was referring to the military term of calling down artillery on top of your own position as a last-ditch effort for survival.

"Exactly," I replied. Then, I held Cassandra's eye with mine in an attempt to steady her. "They're all in there? The witches?"

I waited as patiently as I could with the growing onslaught pounding outside, sapping away my strength. Finally, she nodded ever so slightly, as if ashamed.

"Can you summon them?" I asked.

She nodded again.

"I am their avatar in this world. I can call on one to take my place, come to my aid..." The rest of the words stuck in her throat. She took a breath to clear them and continued speaking. "She will take my place." She looked regretfully down at the cement floor. "But then I cannot come back."

I do not let people close to me. When I have, I invariably lose them, and time does not always heal the wounds. Yet, it was impossible to deny just how fond Cassandra and I had become of each other since Los Angeles. She loved to dance. Many times, she took the lead as we moved our way across the floor. I was going to need her to do it again.

"Unless they summon you back," I offered.

She gave a sad laugh. "Why would they ever do that?"

Suddenly, I gasped and fell forward slightly. The sigils had bunched together, and I could feel their weight on my chest. This was their own Alamo.

"You have to trust me, Cassandra. I will not let them take you from me."

She whispered something for me to remember. I lifted her chin with my hand. Looking into her eyes, I could see her panic and dread at what lay ahead.

"Don't lose hope."

"It will take me a moment —" she took in a deep breath and released it. "To do the summoning."

I rose to my feet. Rowdy and Jo came up beside me.

"Well, what do you know," Rowdy said. "We've got a moment in us left to give."

WE BARELY GOT OUT THE DOOR.

WITH A MASSIVE SWING OF HIS STAFF, DAMARCHUS SENT ME to one knee. A second blow put me down to the cobblestone street. My body was soaked in sweat from the fight, and the sigil glow shrouding it was fading. My shields were useless, and my power was almost gone. Rowdy and Jo came forward, but it was nothing but a cursory gesture. The two were weak, quickly subdued by the lychan horde, and held in place.

Damarchus took his sweet time coming over to me. He was humming a happy tune and smiling as he knelt in front of me.

"Those are some glasses you've got, Black," he said, cocking his head to look at them. "Not even a scratch."

"All the better to see you with," I said.

"If it weren't me, it would have been one of the others, you know. So many bad feels we had in that stuffy little place where they held us. How we hated you."

"What would you be without me?" I asked, glaring back at him with all the defiance my battered face could muster. "Nothing. Meaningless. Like you are now."

"Nothing?" Damarchus struck me with the staff. "Meaningless?"

The head of the staff whistled in its rage as it hammered against me again. I hoped I had bought enough time. Time and I were old friends. Hope, as well.

Damarchus pulled my hair back and studied my bloodied face. "So, how do you think it will feel to finally die, Avery Black?"

"You tell me," I said.

I glanced behind me at the door. Damarchus questioningly followed my gaze to where Cassandra stood. As battered as she was, she had never looked so beautiful. Then, she flung out her arms.

The world exploded into shimmering, blinding, energized light, and fair Cassandra disappeared. Baba Yaga replaced her. Her Russian face was a twisted mask of horror and putrescence. Her near toothless mouth was a darkened, foul maw. A vile, centuries-old creature of legend, she flew into the courtyard in her stone mortar, pestle in hand. Evil was in her wake, looking for prey.

At the sight of her, Damarchus Hill stumbled backward. He tried to raise his staff to Yaga as if raising his hands to block out a scene in a scary movie. However, he had bought the ticket. Now, he got the show.

"Insipid, little cursed boy," Baba Yaga laughed.

With a single swipe of her gruesome hand, Damarchus was turned to bones and dust. Nothing and gone. Blink of an eye. Then, like puppets cut from their strings, the bitten fell where they stood and reverted to human, shaken but alive. Baba Yaga laughed again. A throaty, unholy sound, almost as bad as the howl of the werewolves had been.

Rowdy and Jo pulled themselves up beside me.

"Now that's a cackle," Rowdy said, staring at the witch as she spun inside her ghost gray mortar, soaking in the real world around her. "Out of the frying pan…"

His heavy brow creased with worry and his pupils dilated as his sights shifted from Baba Yaga over to me.

"This was your plan? Replace the horrifying guy with a horrifyinger lady?"

"No," I said, getting to my feet. "This is my plan."

I stepped up to her, and she turned her glaring gaze upon me. Her yellow eyes appraised me. Then, her crooked teeth exposed as she grinned, finding me wanting.

"To think them scared of the likes of you!" she said. Her Russian came out in gobs of spit. "Beaten to death, what hope do you have against…"

I stretched out my hand, palm upturned. In it was a single coin – the one I took out of the man's pocket just before our last stand.

"Payment for your help from an honorable soul," I offered.

Baba Yaga eyed it with greed and anger. Then, she snatched it from my hand. I stretched out my other hand and showed her the second coin.

"I would like Cassandra back now," I said.

Baba Yaga burst out into laughter. A long, raking noise, her sagging breasts heaved beneath her shabby garments. She lifted her pestle high, eyes filled with triumph, and called her magic down on me. Perhaps she meant to turn me to dust and bone as she had done to Damarchus just moments ago.

Nothing happened.

Time to end it.

"You are Baba Yaga. An honorable soul with payment you do not harm. Have you forgotten that?"

She started to answer, but I was having none of it now. I had had my fill of evil.

"Do you know who I am, old hag?" I grabbed her wrist and wrested the pestle from her grip. The shock on her face was total. She tried to pull away, but I moved into her. "I was there when Rome burned, and Nero played. As Khartoum fell. As the Nazis slaughtered."

Baba Yaga shook and tried to bat me away, but I grabbed her other wrist.

"Every cry for hope which echoes in my ear is answered with my hand." I was inches from Baba Yaga's face. I could see the horror she so freely gave to others was now present in her eyes. "Take your payment and give me Cassandra, you long-forgotten horror, or I will pass through The Doorway and erase your memory for all time as if wiping chalk dust from a slate."

Teeth gritted, I told her what Cassandra had whispered in my ear the last time I held her: "I am what Fear fears."

Then, with a flash of golden light, I held Cassandra's face in my hands once again.

THE DOORWAY DID NOT APPEAR.

I KNEW IT WOULD NOT. THERE WAS UNFINISHED BUSINESS TO be attended to here in those weeks in 1888 London.

We stayed on Baker Street in the home of an old colleague who was away investigating a canine incident in England's West Country. Although we had the scent of the man we were pursuing, it took time for Jo and Rowdy to track it. Even with their uncanny sense of smell, the London of this time was foul with pollution, both human and industrial.

It took two weeks to be sure, but the trail eventually led me to open the door and confront the surgeon inside. He was working on a dissection when I entered. He turned from where he was standing across the room, and his eyes narrowed when he recognized me. Then, he raised what had become known throughout history as his weapon of choice; a scalpel.

I held out the hat he had left behind when he had leaped through the window to escape us.

"Jack, I believe this belongs to you," I said.

EPILOGUE

SHE STARED IN DISBELIEF AS THE BRILLIANT ENERGY LIT THE room. Stared in shock at Cassandra when she appeared in her seat at the table an instant later.

Stared in horror as Baba Yaga disappeared from hers.

The Cabal leader stalked quickly around to the Greek girl.

"We agreed you would stay at Black's side until…" She stopped talking as she studied the once beautiful woman who was now covered in blood and sweat. Her gown was threadbare, nothing more than a rag. "Damarchus was meant to kill the werewolf boy. Nothing more."

"I think –" Cassandra paused to find the right words. "I think Rowdy would say, 'he missed the memo.'"

Then, she laughed, and the Cabal leader knew something had changed in the plan – the perfectly thought-out plan.

The witch took a measured breath in an attempt to clearly articulate her words through the anger welling up inside her. Then, grasping the back of Cassandra's chair, knuckles turning pale white, she sweetened her tone.

"Why did you call upon Baba Yaga?" she asked through clenched teeth.

Cassandra glared up at the Witch of Witches, whose evil machinations had become legend through human history and lore. But then, she felt a tingle. The energy was growing. She knew in her heart, in her heart of hearts, that he had been true to his word. Cassandra would give her all, her life, her soul, for the man named Avery Black.

She lifted a single finger to the sorceress' face. It was the finger Rowdy had told her really pissed people off.

"Ask her yourself," she said.

Brilliant light once again engulfed the room. Then, Cassandra was gone, and Baba Yaga was back.

"Noooooooooo!" the woman yelled.

She crushed the back of Cassandra's chair into splitters. Then, she raised a fist, white-hot, a mystic hammer ready to bring down the heavens and turned her wrath on Baba Yaga. With one backhanded slap, she sent her to the floor.

The room was silent save for Baba Yaga's whimpers. No one dared utter a word. Even the coven leader said nothing because there was nothing left to say. Dragon and wolf had not been powerful enough. It was time to call upon something that could not die from sword or spear.

The Cabal sorceress looked to the darkest end of the room as if it contained the answer. It was a place where inner blackness dwelled; the light had never touched it. Then, she made a beckoning motion, and from that place came a deathly cold wisp of air. Icy dread permeated the room as a ghost mask emerged and floated toward the brazier on an unfelt breeze. Its blood-red lips did not move, and its dark eyes were a simple, hollow void.

It was horror. Soulless. Inhuman. Horror.

"Bring. Me. Black," the sorceress said to the spectral manifestation.

It did not respond. Instead, it reached its bone-white hands out above the brazier, its skin taking in the flame's warmth. Then, it was gone.

TURNING JAPANESE

PROLOGUE

I will kill him slowly. No matter what the English witch told me.

I will kill him, not with the knife, but the old way. It has been too long, and my hunger is too great. So, I will peel him back a layer at a time until I reveal everything he had been and everything he had desired and all that was yet to be. Then, like so many men before, I will lay waste to him. Let him end shrieking as I did, in the winter snow so many years…enough.

I await him beyond his doorway – lurk just beyond his reach. The English witch said that he had his protectors, but he who cursed me has his own. They are ancient and formidable, strong in their darkness. They will come, and they will be ended.

I raised my fist. The nails bit into my skin. Blood runs. Delicious pain. I pulled back my knuckles, pure and white, tinged with the blood, and moved them forward.

AVERY:
THERE WAS A KNOCK AT THE DOORWAY.

I ANSWERED IT. 118AD. NORTHERN BRITTANIA.

I was met by the acrid smell of smoke and soot as I entered a battlefield strewn with the debris of combat. Shields. Swords. Spears. Bodies. I moved through the carnage as buzzards and flies descended to begin their work. The armor was Roman. Their standard was cracked and half-buried in the dirt, its red banner that read, *LEG-VIIII HISPANA* lay limp and in tatters on the ground. Men cried out for aid. In the distance, I could hear the dying sound of the battle, Roman legionnaires falling back in a last stand against their Caledonian adversaries.

I went over to one soldier lying upon the ground and lifted his head for us to speak.

"Are you...with...the relief column?" he asked.

He was lucid, though his voice cracked, and blood covered his lips.

"No," I said. "I am your only relief."

I had born this sorrow many times. It had never become easy, and it never seemed to show an end.

The legionnaire's eyes dimmed. Then, he found strength, and he pulled me to him.

"They had been testing…us. Our…resolve. We had to…" he coughed, blood coming with it. "…make our stand."

His words echoed what I had been feeling these last few months with every knock on The Doorway. Instead of bringing Hope, I felt only peril hidden behind the turning of the knob. I found myself questioning what I could do. What difference I made. Yet, The Doorway had still led me here – led me to this.

"How many of you remain?" I asked the soldier.

"A hundred…maybe two," he murmured.

Not enough to make a difference. But perhaps…

"Make for the coast," I told him. "Pull your men together and escape as night falls." He was wounded but strengthened by my presence. "Take to boats and go. Do not give up." I brought him to his feet and saw him become steady, perhaps hearing the fighting of his command not far off. "Do not doubt. Never. Doubt."

"What of The Emperor?" The legionnaire picked up his battered shield and grabbed the Ninth Legion flag from the dirt. "What of Rome?"

I knew why The Doorway had brought me here. It was to give this soldier hope and encourage self-reliance.

"Time to fight for yourself," I said.

ROWDY:
"IT'S A GAME.

Y<small>OU ASK A QUESTION. I ASK A QUESTION."</small>

I finished off what was probably my 50th slice of pizza. I was sitting with Cassandra, but I called her Cass, now. After everything we had been through together in Los Angeles and London, it was like we were on the same team. So, dispensing with the formality of her proper name seemed appropriate. Anyway, Cass was only on her third but savored each bite like a divine moment. She looked radiant sitting across from me in the t-shirt I had bought for her in Times Square. It read: "IT'S ALL GREEK TO ME." In turn, I wore the one she had given me: "TIME IS ON OUR SIDE, YES IT IS." We were having a laugh on June 11th, 1889, drinking beer and eating pizza in what most claimed was the first pizzeria in history.

I motioned to Raffaelle, the creator of this wonderful concoction that would take the world by storm.

"Un'altra strada!" I called to him.

"Mangi iu di un leone!" He smiled back at me then asked, "Piacera alla regina?"

"*Will the queen like it?*" I laughed. "If you only knew!"

Cass wiped the sauce from her lips.

"Asking questions doesn't sound like a game," she said.

I took a swig of beer. "But there's more to it. If you don't answer, you drink. If you do answer, the other person does."

Cass screwed up her nose a bit, trying to figure this out. "But I'm already drinking."

"You have to down the mug."

She nodded, getting it. I motioned for her to go first.

"How many languages do you know?" she asked.

"You're sitting across from a time-traveling werewolf, and THAT'S your first question?" I leaned back in my seat. "I know all of them from Aramaic to Zulu. I can read most of them, too, though some of the early ones can be pretty tough. Sure, ancient caveman looks easy, but telling a mammoth etching from a sloth can be tricky."

"How is that possible?" Cass asked skeptically.

"Sorry. One question at a time. My turn. Down your mug."

She did, and I leaned forward. "Are you a spy for the witches group?"

"They like cabal. Witches' Cabal," she replied.

"Potatoe, potato…are you?"

"No," Cassandra replied flatly.

"No?" I responded.

She smirked. "Did I stutter?"

That was what I got for showing her Breakfast Club.

"If you don't believe me, think a second of who you're playing this game with," she said.

She had me there. I downed my beer as another pitcher arrived.

"Your turn," I said.

"How old are you?" she asked.

"I'm 256 years old," I said, beaming proudly. "Ish." I gave a little hand wiggle with that. "My birthday is in a few weeks, and I'm hoping to get a new Dodger cap since I lost mine in London and they just won the World Series. But how old am I in 'years' years? 'Time' time? How we travel through it? Older. A lot. It's how I've learned all the languages."

Cass drank. She could hold her booze.

"What's it like to be loved by Apollo? A…" I made air quotes. "…a god?"

She sighed. "Gods, Greek gods, at least, are egotistical, overbearing, self-possessed types who find everything they do incredibly amusing. Apollo is like that and knee-weakening handsome while being so."

She took another bite of pizza.

"That's it? C'mon, I want some good stuff!" I said. "A juicy tidbit only I get to know as your friend who takes you to cool spots while Avery's away."

"You want to know about the sex?" she said, seemingly bored. "You and all the sirens. He is…" She paused to consider the wording. "…endowed."

Good enough. I downed my beer.

"Is it true what you said while the werewolves were chasing us in London?" she asked. "If you kill the person who cursed you, your curse will be broken?"

I nodded. "Yeah. That's how I've found it to be. Why?"

She did not answer, but I could see her wheels turning as she drank. She may be the most beautiful chick around, but I found that look unnerving.

"Are you falling in love with Avery?" I asked.

She seemed surprised by the question. Putting down her mug, she eyed me. Then, she smiled, getting the joke.

"He's standing right behind me, isn't he?"

Cass turned, and Avery stood there, smiling down on her. The look on her face could have lit the room. Cass and I had been going everywhere between knocks on The Doorway. She and Avery, too. We had seen Sinatra and Elvis, been to the ballparks, and seen every movie from Casablanca to Avengers. Yet, her and Avery. When they were together, you could feel the magic.

"Are you going to answer or take a drink?" Avery asked.

Silence could speak volumes. There were a lot of volumes speaking for a second. Then, Cass took another long drink. Guess that answered the question.

I was about to ask Avery how the trip was, but he met me with an angry gaze that, frankly, I was pretty happy to see. Someone had been screwing with The Doorway. With us. Enough was enough.

"Well, alright then!" I stood.

Cassandra did the same, a bit confused.

"What's going on?" she asked.

I tossed a huge amount of lira on the table for Raffaelle and put an arm around Cass.

"We are taking the fight to them."

CASSANDRA:
"BUT I WANT TO HELP."

I IMPLORED AVERY.

"I want to be beside you!"

We stood in front of the doorway.

"Then this is the only way," Avery said.

He was stoic, and I was unable to read what he meant.

"We survived Damarchus by the skin of our teeth," he went on. "And that you survived at all is nothing short of a miracle."

I looked to Rowdy.

"The Doorway has taken me to places where I learned every kind of fighting skill known to man," Rowdy said. "It's how I learned all the languages. Hell, I even tried music and painting. It can show you, too, Cass."

"But how long will it take?" I asked reluctantly.

"I cannot tell you that," Avery replied, taking my hand. "The Doorway will know. Time moves like a river. Sometimes rapidly, while at other moments, barely a runal of liquid in the sand. On our side of The Doorway, it can be but a few brief seconds. On yours…"

Avery fixed me with his eyes. I could see my reflection in the polished lenses of his glasses. "You do not have to go."

I hesitated, looking at The Doorway, where Avery's initials were etched in the glass.

"What happens on the other side? Will it change me? Make me something more than I am now?"

"Something different," Avery answered.

"Something better," Rowdy added.

Avery shot Rowdy an irritated look at the remark.

"Different," he said, correcting himself. "More different…er."

I took the knob in my hand. Avery put his hand over mine.

"No matter how long it seems. or how harrowing the journey, we will be waiting when you are ready," he said. "We will answer when you knock."

I smiled weakly at my companions one last time. As a Greek prophet, I believed that they knew; that I knew.

Avery let his hand drop from mine as I turned the knob. Then, opening The Doorway, I crossed the threshold. I felt a blast of cold air; then it closed behind me.

AVERY AND ROWDY STOOD THERE, WAITING.

IT HAD BEEN A SOME MOMENTS SINCE CASSANDRA had walked through the door.

"She gonna slap you or me first when she gets back?" Rowdy asked.

"Both, I would imagine," Avery answered.

"It's gonna feel like a lifetime for her."

"It has felt like a lifetime for me," Avery replied

Another moment passed.

"I liked her the old way. A whole bunch," Rowdy said.

"Me, as well," Avery responded.

"You love her?" Rowdy asked.

And that was when the knock came.

Avery answered The Door.

"SO, IT'S JAPAN," AVERY SAID.

THE RAIN WAS COMING DOWN IN SHEETS OUTSIDE OF SOUTHWICK HOUSE.

"Joy," Rowdy grumbled.

He looked over at Cassandra, who was standing by the window. Her warrior training had changed her. However, considering she had not spoken a word since she had returned, it remained questionable whether it was for good or for bad. The Greek prophet, lover of Apollo, daughter of Troy, was gone, wiped away. Although her face still held remnants of its former loveliness, its aspect had turned cold, and a small scar visible beneath her right eye blighted its perfection. Her green robes had been replaced by a tightly laced black cloth covering her chest and arms. Her shoulders were girded with light shoulder armor plates, and a bamboo woven *karuta* was below her waist. Armed with a bow and a samurai sword, she also packed a *Kusarigama*, a knife with a weighted chain.

Cassandra was now a Japanese *bushi* Samurai.

Avery turned to her. She met his gaze. Yet, her eyes no longer held affection for him. It caused him to inwardly question why he had asked her to go through The Doorway in the first place if it had meant losing her.

"We know it's Japan," he said.

"Because of how The Doorway prepared me," Cassandra stated.

"That is correct. You have been trained as samurai rather than a mage, so I assume you will be guarding me against what lay on the other side of it."

Cassandra responded with one tight nod.

Avery looked to Rowdy. "You know there can be no turning."

Rowdy nodded, disappointed.

"So, he must stay in his human form?" Cassandra questioned.

"Yes," Avery answered.

"Why?" Cassandra asked.

"Because Asian history is rife with possession and curses going back far longer than Rowdy's bite," Avery replied. "Should they take control of Rowdy, with his knowledge and abilities, it could prove to be quite unstoppable."

"That's why I dressed the part," Rowdy remarked.

He motioned to his outfit; head-to-toe spec ops. He was loaded with ammo, M67 grenades, and tactical knives. They were clipped into a Kevlar vest that fit snuggly over his skintight black uniform. His gun belt holstered a semi-automatic pistol, and he had an M556 Microgun slung across his back.

"*Noroi,*" Cassandra said, under her breath. "Curses."

Rowdy picked up a duffel bag by his feet and placed it on a table. He tapped it with his finger.

"Enough C4 explosives inside to rock the house. Just give me the cue, Av – I'll show them what we're made of."

"What we're made of?" Cassandra rebuffed.

"What I'm made of," Rowdy said.

A faint knock came at The Doorway. Cassandra and Rowdy came up to it, flanking Avery.

"What if we open it, and it's just some kid's bedroom or something," Rowdy asked, hoisting the duffel bag over his shoulder.

"Not very likely. You think I wear these glasses for show?" Avery replied.

He called on the sigils of protection. His hands began to glow. Ancient symbols lit across his fingers and along his arms.

Then, he threw open The Door.

AVERY:

WE EMERGED INTO THE MOONLIT OKUNION
CEMETERY IN KOYA-SAN, JAPAN.

THE GRAVEYARD WAS COVERED IN COUNTLESS MOSSED-
covered statues and sculptures that dated back to 800AD.

I looked at Rowdy, who checked his watch.

"Two-thirty on the nose. It's the time the *yurei* roam."

He pulled the pistol and drew the sword. Then, he turned
to me.

"Give me the who and the where," Rowdy said.

"Oldest part of the graveyard," I replied. "If she's here,
she's an ancient power."

Rowdy responded with a small salute and disappeared into
the shadows as if he had never been there at all. Cassandra
drew both of her swords. Their blades were so deeply honed,
they gave off no reflection in the moonlight.

"*Hajimeyou,*" Cassandra whispered in Japanese. She stepped
forward on her heels. "She has arrived."

At the end of the walkway, the *yurei* came into view.
Propelled by a supernatural force, the hem of her white gown

flowed in the low-hanging mist and brushed over the stone markers. Her hair appeared a black drape. Her fingers and arms were like broken branches, and her sharp nails were long and claw-like. It was impossible to tell if she had ever been a ravishing woman because her features were now stretched thin as if in a funhouse mirror.

"Do you find me beautiful?" she asked in Japanese.

The voice was meant to be sweet but came out wrong like something that was once human mimicked the sound.

"You are beautiful to me," I responded.

She turned her face away like a geisha hiding a smile behind a fan.

"You lie…"

A giggle now from her. Its sound was void of mirth or life.

Then, the *yurei* moved closer. I saw a shudder move through Cassandra's body as the apparition stopped a short distance away from her.

"Your protector? From me? I pray you brought more. We are so hungry."

Once more, the giggle. Ghosts acting coy. There is nothing much more frightening than that.

"Not from you." I stepped toward her. "But for you."

Cassandra tried to put herself between me and the *yurei*. I looked at her and, touching her shoulder, gave a reassuring smile.

"Your struggle lies elsewhere tonight, Cassandra."

"Avery, no," she said in English.

A touch of the old Cassandra was evident in her voice.

I turned back to the *yurei*. "You must be all and everything to be in this sacred place, drawing on the souls, tempering their pain and loss."

I lowered my sigils and let them fade.

The *yurei* nodded that she understood. Then, screeching with delight, she plunged into me. My body fell back into the gray granite walkway like a puppet with its strings cut. As my vision dimmed, I saw Cassandra above me. Her feet were bracketing my body, and her swords were poised to let none come near.

CASSANDRA:
HE FELL, AND I STOOD OVER HIM.

THE REPETITIONS. THE MOTIONS. THE PAIN.

Over, and over, and over.

I was forgotten. They were not beyond The Doorway, waiting. Who would be?

Four years, three months, sixteen days.

Over, and over, and over.

Repetition. Motion. Pain.

They were not there.

37,614.

Over, and over, and over.

Repetition. Motion. Pain.

They had forgotten.

2,256,840.

Over, and over, and over.

Yet, I knew why I came here.

Over, and over, and over.

I had not forgotten.

I saw the smoke – watched the *Oni* mask form inside of the wisps. I steadied and stood my ground.

ROWDY:
I KEPT CLIMBING THROUGH THE SHADOWS, HOPING
AVERY AND I WERE RIGHT.

THEN, THE SHADES STARTED TO BREATHE, AND I COULD NOT
believe my luck. I had been itching for a fight, and a fight had
come a-callin'.

Ninjas. Bunches of them. Maybe even oodles. I kept going,
knowing that I was on the right path. When they made their
move, I knew I was in the right place at the right time. There
were heaps of them. Could there be…dare I think it… a ton?

AVERY:
DARKNESS. AN OLD FRIEND OF MINE.

I LET A WICKEN SIGIL OF LIGHT PASS FROM MY FINGERS. IT glowed; turned – barely made a mark against the black before extinguishing.

I turned when I heard the *yurei*. Her face was behind a mask. White. Hollow cuts for eyes, nose, and lips. She shrieked, a wild, maddening howl. Then, she attacked me – flailed at me with her razorblade nails. Her hair whipped like Medusa's snaking locks.

Still screaming, she pushed herself away from me in shocked frustration that I was still standing, untouched.

Away in a place such as we were. A place? A concept. Something better. Closer to the truth. And what was in one's soul but the truth?

"What are you?" the *yurei* asked. "You are not a man."

"No," I replied. "I am not."

She cocked her head, not grasping my response. Then, she perused the surrounding darkness.

"Where have you taken me?" she asked.

"It's where you have taken us," I replied. "Your soul. Your mind. Your heart. Why is it so dark? Why the mask? What do you hide from in your own self?"

"The...mask?"

It referenced it as if not knowing it was there. It touched it but did not take it off.

"Is it masking pain? Anger?" I asked calmly.

She howled and attacked me again; I let it go a moment, then grabbed her arms and shoved her down onto the ground. Her chest was heaving from exertion. Her breath passed through the small opening in the mask. Cold whisps floated and faded. It became cold in that place. I pictured the expression behind the white disguise. Anger. Fear. Confusion.

"Why can...I not...hurt you?" It asked.

I held out my hand. "Give me your mask. What could it hide?"

She shook her head violently, then pointed an accusing finger at me. "What masks do you wear? What do you hide?"

That notion had never occurred to me, but I reached up and touched the sides of my face, anyway. To my amazement, I was wearing a mask. I pulled it off to reveal...myself.

Again and again, I did it, allowing each mask to fall away like dead leaves.

"There is nothing for me to hide from you," I said.

She reached up, and I could hear her sobbing as she took off the mask. I saw gashes that ran high across both sides of her face. Deep cuts, carved by hatred, made into a macabre smile by a vengeful soul.

"Do you find me so beautiful now?" she asked.

She had taken on the form of a woman, a tortured human being. I knelt beside her, and she crawled away from me.

"What snare have you made for me?" she sobbed.

"It's you who have built this cold darkness for yourself. What is your name? I can sense it, but I think you need to say it to end this place for good." I paused and pushed hair from her eyes. "Who did this? End this anger and pain. Who?"

Weeping with shame, she turned her back.

"Why do you care?" The words came out in waves of anguished tears. "Why? Why? No one for centuries has cared!"

"Why?" I asked, puzzled. "Because you knocked on my door."

CASSANDRA:
ITS RED MASK WITH TUSKS LAUGHED AT ME AS WE
ATTACKED AND PARRIED.

EVERY STRIKE FROM THE DEMI-GOD WAS A TWISTING
DISPLAY of force as it wielded its *Kanabo*. The spiked club made
it past my two-sword defense and ripped my bamboo armor
by the knee.

I spun and struck, blades whistled as the air parted before
them, but the beast was gone, and I sliced at smoke. Then, it
reappeared and lashed out from my right. I pulled back and
took a glancing blow to my foot. The pain made me wince. I
retaliated but pierced nothing. It reemerged to my left a
moment later.

Its mask smiled, sensing victory.

AVERY:
SHE LAY THERE WEEPING.

SHE WAS NO LONGER THE SPECTRE THAT KILLED IN vengeance. She was just a scarred, tragic figure, grasping for understanding.

"I was so young. So in love."

A woman now, not a thing, laughed at the concept. The gashes that traced the edge of her mouth did not allow her lips to move.

"He said he loved me. But he was Samurai, a warlord. He was a…liar. Then, when he thought he would be found out, he paraded me out before my family – made me watch as he killed them. And I…" Her voice faltered. "…was made an example. Cut. Deformed. Left to die and cursed in death." Her eyes that could still show hatred at the memory turned icy like her breath. "For love."

"Give me his name. Let me end this injustice done to you. Return you to your family," I said.

"To…my family. You can do such a thing?"

"I did not come to fight you," I said, and let my sigils glow all around me. "I came here to show what I am. What me and my friends are. We came here to save you."

I took her hand, and she gave me his name.

ROWDY:
"ON IT!" I FIGURED IT WOULD BE THIS PLACE ANYWAY.

ALTHOUGH HEARING THE NAME IN MY HEAD FROM AVERY had confirmed it. Biggest mausoleum. Swarming with ninjas. Tough call.

The problem was, the farther in I fought, the better the defense became. One of them tagged me with a hard kick to the rib. Another one put a foot into my jaw that was solid enough to need to see a dentist. Of course, neither of those guys would be kicking anyone ever again, but one had to give them props.

I ran up the stairs beneath the ancient arch. Getting this close, I expected to confront a Black Clad Ninja Rave A Goo Goo, but they all melted away. They left me alone for a whole second and a half with my cracked ribs and throbbing jaw before the ground started to shake like a polaroid peeck-cha.

The first bone smacked me in the back of the head then hurtled past me. The next, a femur, I thought, hit me on the arm. Then, an avalanche of appendages from thousands of graves whistled past me and formed together at the top stairs.

"And this is my surprised face," I said to myself.

Before me, it rose, built from the bones of the early dead here in Okunion. Those in unmarked graves and those from the mountain country nearby who never had a burial. They all assembled around me – a massive *Gashadokuro.*

An unstoppable, unkillable, humungous skeleton guy stood between me, blowing the whole place to another afterlife. All that for trying to save some ghost chick that wanted to rip us to shreds for yucks and giggles. The injustice of it all.

I reached into the satchel and popped the timer cap.

Five minutes and counting down.

Then, I ran right at the deadly thing with a bag filled with explosives and a cocked-to-rock XM556 Microgun.

"C'mon! Everyone in the pool!" I yelled.

CASSANDRA:
A BLOW TO MY BACK BROUGHT STARS TO MY EYES.

BUT I COUNTERED WITH A STAB OF MY BLADE THAT PROVED a severe hit to my ghostly assailant, and I was spared the kill shot. Avery still lay motionless at my feet. Whatever he was doing in the *yurei* netherworld needed to reach its conclusion for us survive.

A raindrop hit my face. Then, another and another. They fell in a quiet rhythm as the next attack came at me from the right. Smoke. It came at my left. Smoke. It vanished, but reappeared. Parry. Parry. Over, and over, and over.

The rain fell on me in a steady tempo, creating a lethal beat that connected my mind with my body. I tenaciously fended off more attacks Front. Left. Right. Behind. I spun stealthily with the smoke and thrust both of my blades out in front of me into what was air one moment, then a demi-god the next. Finally, I felled it. If its malevolent, smiling mask could register emotion, I thought it would be respect.

Then, in a collapsing cloud of vapor, it was gone.

That is when I heard the explosion.

ROWDY:
FOR A BIG GUY, HE MOVED AWFUL FAST.

THE NIGHTMARE SKELETON SLUGGED LIKE A PRIZEFIGHTER and sent me sprawling against the walkway surrounding the mausoleum of some bad guy from who knows what AD. But I knew how to mess with these massively horrifying creatures from a Japanese monster movie.

Get 'em frustrated; they start to overheat.

In the last three minutes, I had shot, smacked, and stabbed this thing into a red glowing frenzy. Then, I popped a few grenades at it and really spiked its fury meter. That was when it overreached with its colossal fist, and I broke for the target. Satchel in hand, I skidded under its pelvis, and using its 30-foot tibia like a stripper pole, I flung the charged explosives into the burial chamber.

…40…39…38…ish…

I made my break for the exit when the Gashadokuro's pinkie caught me in the calf and sent me down.

I was not going to make it.

So, I did what any other crazy person would do with about twelve seconds left to live. I ran straight at its phalanges, leaped on its patella, sprung off its coccyx. Then, grabbing its sternum, I hoisted myself up to scream in its face.

"Sayonara, Skull Boy!"

I pushed off into the air just as the C4 exploded. Then, I rode the shock waves through the sky. Yet, I knew I was not going to stick the landing. There was only thing that could save me…

I began to change.

CASSANDRA:
I WATCHED IN DISBELIEF.

Countless bones, dirt, cement, and one lone figure erupted into the sky.

Rowdy came plummeting down, yelling. He hit the pathway hard, nearly rolling beside Avery's yet unmoving form. Something was wrong. I heard voices. Chants. Echoes. They all raced at Rowdy as he lay on the ground, writhing in some invisible but agonizing struggle.

He was changing as spirits all about latched onto him. They were using his curse and trying to take his power for their own. These were ancient evils even more powerful than Rowdy.

I ran to him. He looked up at me in pain. Still human, but eyes yellowing, teeth extending.

"Kill me, Cass…"

"No!" I took his face in my hands and held his gaze. "You will not let them take you. You will not let them kill in your name."

He was struggling, suffering, so I knew he was still with me, though the spirits of the dead danced all along his flesh and out his mouth and eyes.

"We are the same. Cursed souls. We have work left to do!"

I screamed to be heard over the cries of the dead all around us. Then, I slapped him.

"I need to go to Woodstock!" I slapped him again, harder. "You said you would take me to Macy's!" Then, I reared back an open palm to strike. "You said we would go to Disneylanddddd!"

I brought the blow down with all the strength I had left, and he fell unconscious.

The ghosts went back to whence they came.

Exhausted, I collapsed on top of him. I feared what lay ahead. I questioned whether I had the strength to do what I knew inside needed to be done.

AVERY:
HER EYES FLEW OPEN, AND I KNEW.

ROWDY HAD BROKEN THE CURSE.

I awoke on the walkway. The figure that was a centuries-old spectre of vengeance was now just a woman in my arms. I held her and watched the scars on her face fade away. For a fleeting moment, the beauty that she once was before her life was taken was visible.

"What is your name?" I asked her.

The sun had started to shine just over the mountains that surrounded the cemetery.

"Aiko," she answered softly.

"Little Loved One," I said. "A beautiful name for a beautiful girl."

She smiled. Her features were soft and delicate, becoming transparent. Then, she touched my face with her hand. Japanese sigils raced down my arm as if to comfort her. Protect. Golden repair. All were glowing as they left my fingertips.

"The English woman…" she whispered.

She saw I did not understand. Still, she held my gaze. When she spoke again, her whisper waned with her spirit.

"She sent me to prepare you."

Then, the sunlight caught her cheek. She angled her head to feel warmth.

"So beautiful," she said. Then, she saw something. "Papa? Mother?"

She faded from existence.

I did not cry; it is a peculiarity I have found. Perhaps due to what I am. Perhaps due to what I have seen. But if I could cry, I would have then.

The Doorway appeared behind me.

I had not felt its coming and turning. Then, I realized why. It was not there for me.

Cassandra crossed to it and put a hand upon the knob.

She looked at Rowdy. He was a few feet away from me and just now regaining consciousness. Then, she gazed at me for a long, sad moment.

"I know you wouldn't believe me if I told you I loved you," she said. "No one ever could."

Then, she walked through The Doorway, closing it behind her as the rain continued to fall.

Rowdy was on his feet quickly, looking at The Doorway, then me in total disbelief.

"Can anyone use this thing now?" he asked.

I stood, straightened my glasses, and walked up to Rowdy. He was still smoldering a bit, but otherwise, no worse for wear.

"I believe," I paused, "she was invited to use it."

"Oh. I thought it only worked for you," he replied.

"Me…or the ones who made it."

I raised my hand and rapped on the glass.

The Doorway opened, and we went in.

OLYMPUS:
WINNER TAKES IT ALL

AVERY:
I KNOCKED AND OPENED THE DOOR.

There is a first time for everything.

We were met with was the incredible brightness of the afternoon sun. After coming from the darkness of Okunion Cemetery into the glare of light, Rowdy and I shielded our eyes. Then, squinting them open, we saw the lushness of the green grass at our feet and the richness of a blue, unblemished sky. All so perfect; it was like rendering from a children's book.

"We've died and gone to a Tellatubbie set," Rowdy remarked, taking take it all in.

Then, I saw the woman lying in the grass a distance away from us. She was Grecian beauty who wore her hair tied back in braids. From where I stood, I could see deep finger bruises on her arm that were a stark contrast to her flawless skin. A wooden box was at her feet. It had the Greek letter 'P' on its top panel.

So, it had all come to this.

"All these troubles caused by this man, you say?"

The voice was an echo with an otherworldly timbre. It sounded from behind us.

"I was excepting someone less…scholarly in aspect."

Rowdy and I slowly turned and faced the gods of Olympus. Apollo was dressed in nothing but a red scarf and skirt. He was a perfect specimen who held Cassandra in his arms. She was still outfitted in her samurai armor and dressings, bow in hand. Her expression was stoic, and she conspicuously avoided eye contact with me.

Beside them was Ares, the Greek spirit of battle and god of war. Unlike his brother Apollo, he was dressed for combat, complete with a golden chest plate and armor. His helmet was arched with plumage, and he was armed with shield and sword.

I turned away from the gods and moved to the woman in the grass. Placing my hand beneath her chin, I lifted her face to mine. She smiled weakly. Then, she touched my face and ran her fingers through my hair.

"So proud of you," she said.

Her eyes were filled with memories from long ago, and she smiled. I mirrored her emotion like a son returning home from lands far away.

"Who is she?" Rowdy asked, coming up behind me.

"I believe that she is the closest thing I will ever have to a mother." I made a gesture of introduction between them. "Rowdy, this is Pandora." I motioned to the grass. "And that is her box."

I brought up her arm and called upon a Navajo healing sigil to ease her pain. Unfortunately, it was to no effect.

In the god gathering behind us, Ares spoke up.

"Remind me why I am here, brother," he asked. "Surely, it is not to spend time with these unimpressive half-beings."

"This is where we put an end to all this," Apollo replied.

"Then, get on with it," Ares said.

I turned to them and raised Pandora's injured arm for Apollo to see.

"Is this your doing?"

"Oh, that is the least of her pains for what she's been up to, I assure you." Apollo pointed a finger at Pandora. "I will send her to push with that smiling idiot, Sisyphus for her scheme to give Hope a chance."

Pandora started to speak, but Apollo lifted his chin ever so slightly, and she remained silent.

"The first woman, fashioned with Zeus' blessing, and this is how you repay him? By letting Hope out through some conjuring while our backs were turned?"

Rowdy stared at Apollo like he had escaped from a freak show. Then, he looked at Cassandra.

"You're not seriously be going back to this jerkwad?"

"Jerkwad?" Ares asked, puzzled.

"It must be a term of respect we are obviously not accustomed to, Ares." Apollo kept his attention on Rowdy. "Do not seem so astonished, half-mortal man. This was all Cassandra's idea from the start." He moved the back of his hand along one of her smooth cheeks. "She left me a letter at my temple telling all about what this…" He made a dismissive motion to me. "…manifestation of Hope was doing. We put all those earthly desires in the box for a reason. Pandora let them out and closed Hope within as he desired."

Rowdy was not following. So, Apollo paced his words as though speaking to a child and continued.

"In that way, humanity would cling to us. Since we held their only Hope, their gods and creators would turn to us for their salvation."

"Oh, okay," Rowdy said, as though it was the stupidest idea he had ever heard. "How'd that all work out for you? I think humanity got the better of you on that plan?"

"And because of that, now you have me to deal with me," I said, standing.

"Exactly. So back in the box you go," Apollo replied.

"Over my dead body!" Rowdy suddenly realized what was going on and charged forward, transforming into his lychan form before I could stop him.

Cassandra drove into him as Apollo recoiled. Rowdy and Cassandra pushed into each other, faces mere inches apart. Then, Cassandra said something to him, but he shoved her away and launched himself at the gods bearing his razor-sharp claws and fangs.

Ares snatched him out of the air like a fly and held Rowdy at arm's length, studying him, amused by his ferocity.

"I thought you might like it," Apollo said offhandedly to Ares. "Cassandra mentioned him in her letter. Maybe make it a war toy of yours or something."

"No!" I yelled.

"You have no powers here! Your sigils and symbols are from tribes and clans that have never been! You are nothing without their…" Apollo looked at Cassandra, trying to remember. "What was your word from the letter?" He thought a moment. "Yes! Belief! You are nothing without their belief!"

"Why, Cass? Why would you do this to us?" Rowdy snarled, trying fruitlessly to break Ares' grip.

At that, Cassandra looked into my eyes for the first time, but did not speak.

"I lifted her curse. She is with me again. Awash in my love," Apollo said.

Then, he was upon me in an instant. He grabbed me by the hair and lifted me as I struggled against him. Then, Pandora's Box opened, and I was pulled into it.

It was over in a heartbeat.

Pandora's Box slammed shut.

CASSANDRA:
I REMEMBER WHEN I BECAME ME.

I HAD BEEN SOME KIND OF CHARACTER, A WARNING THAT A woman should be happy with what she was given or face the consequences. I was loved by a god, a beautiful one, who bestowed me gifts if only I would…what? Pretend to love him? Hang on his arm? Laugh at his comments and serve his needs?

When I saw what Apollo would make of me, I said 'no'. Henceforth, I was never to utter a word that would be believed or be taken as truth. And my heart would never know another's as the words from my mouth would betray me. I was cursed forever.

But I found me in the shadow of Mount Kusatsu- Shirane, under the Family Shimadzu, in 12th century Japan. My life was a set of rituals. Of repetition. With weapons. With words. With silence. An endless series of these that asked me to fail from it. To surrender to it. To give up on what I thought I could do and see what I may well accomplish. I asked my body to move when it was no longer able. I forced myself to continue when

I believed that I could not. And I was told to remain silent. Ever silent. But this was not when I became me.

A woman painted me on a silk scarf one day as I trained. It had been so long since I had seen my own image, I no longer knew what I looked like. In her rendering, the mountain rose behind me, and my hair burned red like a flame as it fell down my back and against my green kimono. I held my blade up and out. Steady. Prepared. Not a different me. Or a better me.

A discovered me.

I did it all and would again to lift my curse. All so I could tell the man I had fallen in love with that I loved him and have him believe me.

ROWDY:
I SERVE AT HIS DESIRE.

HIS WEIGHT UPON MY BACK MAKES ME LONG FOR BLOOD.
For battle. For pain. For victory.
For Ares!

AVERY:
I WAS IN THE DARKNESS AGAIN.

I SAT, IF ONE COULD CALL IT THAT, IN A BOX THAT SEEMED TO have no dimensions. Alone, I culled my thoughts, piecing together what had happened, attempting to understand.

Cassandra looked at me when Apollo said…

"Hello…"

The voice was that of a little boy – curious and innocent. It was near to me, almost beside me.

"Hello," I answered.

"Are you the one who answers my knocking?"

"Your knocking?" I asked.

"Yes. Mother, the woman who speaks to me from outside; she said if I knock on the lid, hopefully, someone will answer."

"Hopefully," I said, amused by the boy's choice of words.

"I know when people are in need, so I knock."

"I answer," I told him.

"Does it make a difference? Do you make a difference?"

The boy seemed excited at the prospect of it.

"I try to."

I could sense him nodding, trying to understand.

"The others that left can be very strong. Power, Hate, and Revenge."

"Yes, they can."

"Mother said they had to go because I needed all the room," the boy explained. "People may follow the others call outside, but they all need me inside."

I thought about that for a moment.

"Hope?"

"Yes," the young voice answered.

"I always thought I was you," I replied.

Rollicking laughter cut through the darkness. It went on and on like music flowing into my soul.

"Me?" Hope said finally. "I make them look up from their hunger, but you make them pick up the plow! I made them get up from the mud, but you got them to man the battlements!" His voice was like an anthem. Rousing. Inspiring.

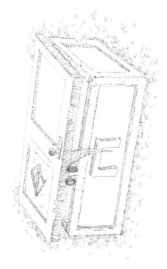

"You're what the tiniest spark of me sets alight! You're the one who opens The Doorway to Possibility."

Now, I knew why Cassandra had looked at me – why she had brought us here.

But the question was, could I get us out?

SACAJAWEA:
I TRACKED THE DEER FOR HALF THE DAY.

I WATCHED AS THE DOE GRAZED AMONGST THE FIR AND PINE trees along the banks of the Umpqua River. The hum of its waters' downward flow in the distance helped mask my approach to the animal so that, even when I was at arm's length, it continued to eat, undisturbed.

My bone knife was sheathed, so I posed no threat to it today. Reaching out my hand, I touched the doe's flank. It lifted its head and pricked its ears, but made no motion to bolt. Instead, it looked at me, unafraid. I stared into its dark eyes and stroked its fur. Then, I heard Rowdy call to me. I looked around, but he was not there. A moment passed, and the forest became very still. Finally, he said my name again. It sounded as if he was close behind me. I turned quickly. The deer spooked and bounded away.

"Rowdy!" I cried out.

Only the silence of the trees answered.

ROWDY:
I FELT MYSELF SLIPPING AWAY.

TRY AS I MIGHT, AS HARD AS I FOUGHT, IT WAS A LOST CAUSE.
Ares had changed me into his were-steed and used his
Grecian god powers to shape my lychan form to his will. I was
now as big as a horse, my talons a foot long, my fangs even
longer. He rode on my back in a saddle of gold and let out a
bloodthirsty cry as he carved his way through the opposing
army before him with his sword. We were at the Battle of
Chaeronea. The Greek army was fighting the Macedonians in
what would be their fall to Alexander the Great. That was how
it had played out historically, but now, maybe not. With Ares
and I, the course might change.

The two of us together were a whirlwind of destruction,
and men fell before us like wheat to a scythe. I slashed and
clawed, insane with the lust for battle Ares drove into my skull.
Words like rend, slash, kill, and blood streamed through my
consciousness. I could not stop them. Avery and I had studied
every kind of mental manipulation, but whatever Ares had
done to me did not feel like an attack at all. Instead, he had
tapped into my lychan blood, the one that craved the hunt and
hungered for the kill. I frothed at the bit and strained against

the reins, eager to dive into the fray. Yet, the part of me that was human held Sacajawea's face in my mind. I focused on her and made a desperate plea for her help. I yearned to get back to her, but with every death I caused, her image faded from my memory.

SACAJAWEA:
THE CALLING HAD BEEN A GHOST CRY ON THE WIND.

I SUDDENLY FELT ROWDY'S PAIN IN MY MIND AS IF IT WERE my own, and I was overwhelmed by his sense of doom. My heart clamored in desperation; Rowdy had always faced danger with a laugh. Yet, this was something else; this felt like a death. I knew that I must act quickly and contact him.

Black had once shown me a sign that allowed him to traverse dimensions and communicate with all people. Could it work here so that I could somehow reach my mate across time? I knelt and grabbed at the earth and the leaves around me.

"Yaawisen."

I told myself to hurry as I completed the ring around me.

"Nasundanwah."

I remembered that Black had drawn an egg shape that surrounded a moon. Now, I clawed my fingers into the dirt to create a circle with me at its center, and I called to Rowdy. Still, I heard nothing in reply. Then, I looked at the symbol and saw what I had forgotten. I added streaking lines reaching outward from the egg to complete it. Taking out my bone knife, I cut my finger. My gaze steeled downward at what I had scrawled, I watched my blood fall onto the sigil in thick drops.

Black had said the last step to empower it was the most difficult. I had to believe. Drawing in a breath deep within my chest, I shut my eyes and screamed my soulmate's name.

ROWDY:
I HEARD MY NAME.

THE SOUND OF IT PIERCED THROUGH THE BLOODLUST THAT had all but consumed me.

"Rowdy!"

The voice blared in my mind. *Jo? Was that Jo?*

Then, I charged into the Macedonian ranks, which were now beginning to break. I was a wild thing now, my human self all but gone.

"Rowdy! I am here with you!"

It was Jo! She had somehow heard me. I could feel her – sense her with me. I stopped fighting, and Ares reared me, slapping my hindquarters with the flat of his sword, trying to get me back into battle. Slapping my hindquarters? That is my ass he was whacking!

I spun my head around to face him, and I saw the realization in his eyes that he had lost control of me. He raised his sword, its brutish, gouged blade pitted and stained. He brought it down at my neck. At the same moment, I opened my massive jaws to bite. It was going to come down to a millisecond. Ares, Greek God of War versus Richie Crowe, a werewolf with a heart of gold, winner takes it all.

I caught his sword arm an inch from my skin and drove my fangs in deep. Ares howled in pain. Not wanting to cut that sound off anytime soon, I wrenched him from his saddle and flung him back into his men, his sword falling to the ground between us. Snarling, I bit through the leather straps holding the saddle on my back and chucked that in the war god's face for good measure.

"Rowdy!" Jo's anguished cry echoed in my mind.

I concentrated on her voice and used its timbre as a mighty staff to break the bonds of Ares' waning spell on me. I could feel him resisting, then refusing to let me go. Still, I focused on Jo. Her power and love were a greater strength.

"I'm here, Jo!"

I spoke the words out loud, and suddenly, I reverted to my human self. I was not a hundred percent, but each call of my name from Jo made me that much stronger. I could see her somehow, kneeling in the forest, tears streaming down her face.

"Don't cry. You saved me," I said as if she were beside me.

In my mind's eye, I saw her tense body relax; her head fell forward in exhaustion.

"I'm okay," I told her. "The Greek god of war is trying to kill me right now, but it's not as bad as it sounds. Talk in a sec."

Ares rose to his feet; the wound on his arm was already healing itself.

"I will drag your corpse through my ranks, welp! Bask in your cries as I turn you into a carpet!"

He did not beat around the bush. One had to appreciate that kind of boasting from a guy who did not know what he had stepped in, and on, was me. Still, I had to admit Ares was a big one, easily ten feet tall, which worked in my favor because it made him overconfident. Of course, having come out on top in countless fights throughout eternity probably made him overconfident, too. That was going to make the next few minutes all the better.

All around us, the battle raged on. We circled one another. He made a play to grab his sword lying in the dirt. It was closer to me, though, and as he was about to close his hands on the leather grip, I snapped a spinning side kick into his face that broke his nose and sent him stumbling back.

"That's a *usiro ura mawashi geri*, Ares – toughest kick in the world to master. Let me show it to you again."

I moved forward. Shocked from the first blow, Ares brought up his fists in defense of his face. So, I planted my foot directly in his crotch. The armored flap covering it made a ringing noise, but the blow was solid. I could feel every man within earshot wince. Ares groaned and sank to one knee.

"That's the bell!" I held my hand to my ear as if to listen. "Class is now in session."

I reached down and hoisted Ares' sword from the dirt, my fingers barely fitting around the grip.

That was when it spoke.

"I am the sword of Hephaestus," it said. "Who wields me, warrior? Anoint me with a name, and you will have my power."

A talking sword – got to love the gods, right?

"Give me my blade!" Ares bellowed and charged me. I sidestepped the attack but was too slow to dodge the swipe of his right arm as he passed. Then, he locked me in a bear hug and forced me down into the grass. The sword was now between us, inches from each other's neck. He leaned his weight into me, bringing back his fist to deliver to deliver a death blow to my head.

"Time to die, mortal boy," he growled.

I grinned up at him. "Yeah? Watch this. Don't blink, or you'll miss it."

I swung my right leg out, let my left shoulder down, and pushed my hips up. Ares lost his balance, and I twisted him onto the ground to where I had been a second before. Then, I jumped back on my feet and gave him a good ol' fashioned kick in the chin for good measure. Snatching the sword from the dirt, I held it up so its blade caught the sunlight and called out so all could hear.

"I am Rowdy of House Crowe! I call you Shoshoni, after the house of my wife who saved me!"

In my hand, the blade transformed. It morphed, apparently making itself match the characteristics of its bearer. Its blunt, rough edges tapered out and grew smooth. The grip lengthened above the guard, and the pommel twisted into the shape of an S. Then, its mystical power surged through me and imbued me with a greater sense of justice, courage, and honor. I suddenly felt like a knight.

I leveled it at Ares and spoke in ancient Greek, just so there were no misunderstandings between us.

"I am a paladin of time, Ares. I've known combat since the first shove. Every tick of the clock has been my classroom."

I motioned the god to his feet with the tip of the blade. His war mace was still looped on his saddle, so I gave it a nod, never taking my eyes off him.

"C'mon, Goliath. Meet your David," I challenged.

Ares grabbed his mace. Despite his bleeding nose, aching groin, and bruised ego, he came at me. His first attack was a clumsy overhand strike followed by a slow-moving swing and an off-balanced thrust. I parried, feeling the elegance of my new broadsword in my hand. Perfectly weighted, it seemed to anticipate my every move.

Now it was my turn. I smashed away his mace with a discarded shield. Then, I attacked his body's nerve clusters using Muay Thai from Thailand. It struck his pain centers with a fallen spear like it was a Japanese Shikomizue. I planted my foot on his chest, backflipped off it, and in mid-air let Shoshoni slice through his breastplate from the buckle to the throat. I even stuck the landing. I was a Baryshnikov of battle. A Picasso of pain. A Mickey Mouse of… mayhem?

Ares fell to the ground bleeding and raised a single hand raised in surrender. The fight was over. Shoshoni faded away, but I could ever so slightly feel its weight still on my fingers, ready at a moment's notice to reappear.

"Sit," I told Ares. "Stay."

I surveyed the chaos of the battlefield. Finally, I saw who I was searching for riding toward me on a burly warhorse.

"Hey! Alex! You can take it from here! Start your greatness!" Then, I turned my face to the sky. "Zeus! How was the view? Release my friends, or I'm going to sushi-up your son and serve him with wasabi!"

And like that, we disappeared.

CASSANDRA:
APOLLO GOT OUT OF BED AND YAWNED.

Then, he smiled at me like I should burst into applause from where I lay in the rumpled sheets.

A moment later, his smile faded as he looked out at the new dawn. Then, stretching, he let his muscles ripple before picking up his Lyre. He played his fingers along the strings and fixed his sights on Pandora's Box. Its polished wood caught the morning sunlight from where it sat on the balcony. I had to find a way to get Avery out there, but Apollo had not let me near it since the day before.

A knock came at the door, and a servant girl entered with an object on a small pillow. She handed it to Apollo and was quickly dismissed. I watched as Apollo held it up to the light. It was adorned with the letter *P* in gold, with Apollo's Lyre symbol below it.

"This should do nicely," Apollo said matter of fact.

"Is that?"

"A lock. One for which there is no key."

He crossed over to the box. He looked down on its engravings before shifting his gaze to me.

Despite my concentrated stoicism, I must have given something away, for he quickly pulled me off the bed and dragged me over to Pandora's Box. Then, he grabbed me by the hair and thrust the lock into my hand.

"Loop it through the ring and close the hasp for good. Done will be done," he commanded.

I kept my gaze down. I could not bear to look at the box with the thought of locking it for eternity. My hopes were quickly fading away of ever being with…

"Never lose Hope. Never stop believing."

The whisper was in my mind.

"Why do you hesitate, Cassandra?" Apollo asked. He pushed me down farther toward the box. "Curse you for ever showing your face to me."

"No," I said, "Curse you, I believe."

I flung the lock at him and threw open Pandora's Box.

Avery exploded from within in a cascade of sigils, signs, and markings collected throughout time. He seemed constructed of them as they swam about his body. An angel of Hope, no longer shackled to a myth and harnessed in the darkness. He was strong in his Belief.

Apollo grabbed his bow. He had an arrow nocked by the time Avery turned to him with the Greek god's symbols of power, from Hestia's Fire to Poseidon's Trident, exploding from his glowing form. He tore the weapon from Apollo's hand. Stunned, Apollo circled away from him. Avery mirrored his movements until they faced off. Then, a portal opened, and Ares was flung through it, bloody, beaten, and bewildered.

"Get this cursed beast away from me!" he yelled.

Rowdy stepped through the porthole behind him. He was in human form and covered in the god's blood. He pointed a warning finger at Ares.

"Climb on my back again —" he pointed a warning finger at Ares. "And I'll give you another serving of whoop-ass, this time with a side of ranch!"

Then, Rowdy looked around the room and was taken aback by what he saw.

I was naked.

Avery was glowing and floating a few feet off the floor.

Apollo and Ares were pressed against a back wall.

"Did I come at a bad time?" he asked.

"Just one moment, Rowdy," Avery said.

He glided across the room, and the energy he radiated melted the tiled floor beneath him. He stopped before Apollo and Ares. His were sigils glowing angrily to match his mood.

"We are taking the box and leaving. You are not to bother us again." He pointed to Apollo. "And you will never harm Pandora or Cassandra, or I will use The Doorway and turn your very existence to nothingness."

Zeus, and a company of other Greek gods, appeared on the balcony as he spoke. Avery then turned to face him.

"You understand that if that happens, there will be no more songs. No victories. Nothing. Then, you will be forgotten by the mortals," Avery said.

Rowdy and I came over to stand with him as the two sides squared off. Zeus scowled back at Avery, then he glanced at Pandora's Box and nodded. And with that, the gods were gone.

Rowdy gave a fist pump. "And the winner takes it all!"

I quickly grabbed for my armor and weapons as Avery's glow subsided. Then, Rowdy clapped him on the shoulder, and the two shared a bro hug.

"How did you get free of Ares?" Avery asked.

"Jo saved me," Rowdy replied. "I don't know how she did it, but it's a good thing – I had full-on gone to the dark side with Ares."

"My bursting from the box buttressed all of our beliefs while at the same time dispelling theirs," Avery explained. "They are nothing without those who believe in them."

Now clothed and armed, I walked back over to stand beside them. Rowdy looked at me with smirk.

"Five seconds – kicked Ares ass in like five seconds. You want to hear about it?" he asked.

I tightened the sash around my waist and tied back her hair.

"I'm sure we will never stop hearing about it," I replied, and looked to Avery. "I knew you were more than what could fit in that simple box."

At that, Avery smiled and took me in his arms.

I sighed at his touch. "If I told you I loved you, would you believe me?"

"Yes."

We kissed. I hoped it would be something we did over and over and over.

EPILOGUE
AVERY:

A<small>T THAT VERY MOMENT, BANGING BEGAN AT THE</small> D<small>OORWAY.</small>

It was a desperate, rapid pounding.

"Well, that doesn't even remotely sound promising," Rowdy said.

He started into his lychan transformation as Cassandra nocked an arrow. I let my sigils of attack and protection come forward on my fists and arms. Then, I opened The Door, and a woman in red fell into my arms. Her black hair was sweaty tangles across her shoulders and down her back. Her face was a mask of panic and shock. She clung to me, grasping at my arms and clothing as if her life depended on it.

"Black!" she cried. "It's too late!"

Her eyes were wide, pupils pinpoints of fear as she gestured around her.

"I tried to prepare you. I sent the dragon, the wolf, and the ghost," she rambled. "But he knew of my machinations and struck without warning! It all happened so fast. We have run out of time!"

Suddenly, chaos swarmed around us. Knights on horseback clashed swords. Archers let loose high volleys arrows; men fell to their deaths.

Rowdy looked at a burning castle under siege in the background. Its red and black Pendragon banners were being set ablaze. Then, he looked back at me.

"Tell me that isn't Pendragon as in Arthur Pendragon," Rowdy said.

"Son of Uther the Lightbringer – I'm afraid so," I replied.

"So, just to be clear, this is –"

"Camelot."

End of the World
As We Know It

PROLOGUE:
MORGANA LE FAY SAT BEFORE A SCRYING POOL IN HER
CHAMBER.

SHE THOUGHT OF HER SON, MORDRED. HE WAS READY AND fit. He was prepared to lead an army against the castle and the king. When that happened, she would then bring the Black Wizard and his Doorway to her. Then, once the battle was over, Time would be at her feet.

In total, she had sent the Dragon and had tried to kill his paladin with the werewolves. Then the ghost woman was dispatched to draw the information from his soul of where he had sent the girl. Unfortunately, all these endeavors to thwart Avery Black's magic had failed.

Still, the girl named Eve existed. She was the knower of all things since time began. She was the key to…

Morgana was suddenly distracted by the scrying pool in the center her room. Its clouded surface swirled then showed the face of her son, Mordred. She looked at him, bewildered. He was dressed in her armor and clad for battle.

"Mother," Mordred said, mounting a steed. "I do not know how you convinced them, but their army has formed on me.

Legions. We have begun the movement of the siege towers and archers. The king had no time to escape."

He sounded elated.

What army? Morgana Le Fay thought. She and she alone had planned all this. But this was not to her timing. She looked down at the pool. At the image of her son, the future king of all and everything, trying to piece it all together.

Then, she heard someone at her door.

"Who is there?!" she snarled.

"It is you."

The voice was her own.

Morgana Le Fay's first thought was that it was a ruse of dark magic meant to annoy her. Then, a flood of water exploded through the door's hinges, ripping it from its frame and cresting her face. It brought with it a rumble of slippery stones that sent her to the ground. She looked up at the water's surface and the rippling image of herself.

"Your son will lead my army, and my son will rule The Table." She leaned her face into the water and clearly spoke. "Merlin will not answer your summons, stupid woman." She began to laugh. "I have put him where he will no longer matters – encased in amber. He is no longer on the board."

Morgana Le Fay scrambled to the reach air. She looked around and saw the woman standing right in front of her. She was herself, still laughing as she basked in her turning the screws that would make her the Queen of All and Everything.

"Bring to me The Wizard of History. Bring me the girl to shape Everywhere and Everywhen to my will." She twirled, and water fanned about the chamber until she became one with it. "It's the end of the world as we know it – and I feel fineeee!"

AVERY:
THE DOORWAY HAD BROUGHT US THERE TOO LATE.

CAMELOT WAS UNDER SIEGE. TREBUCHETS WERE LAUNCHING fiery boulders covered in tar at its battlements. Arrows darkened the sky as volleys were launched over the battlefield. Cavalry and pikemen fought in a flow across the open ground. The air was heavy with smoke and the noise war, but as staunchly as the kingdom's defenders fought to save their castle, they were fiercely outnumbered by their assailants. I could see at once that the kingdom would be lost.

I had raised my sigils of protection, both Norse and Germanic, in hopes of buying us a few precious moments that would reveal our mission. The fight raging around us was at its crescendo. In the face of such opposition, I knew my signs could not hold much longer.

"Well, it's not the Monty Python version. No coconuts for horses," Rowdy called to me over the commotion. "No singing, so probably not Lerner and Loewe's musical. Could be White or Mallory's take on the place."

"We are here now," I hollered back. "I believe that makes it our own."

Rowdy dispatched two attackers charging toward us. However, more were behind them, ready to confront the threat of our presence.

I turned to Morgana Le Fay. She was on the ground, having wormed her way behind us as though we were her shield.

"Where is King Arthur, Le Fay?" I demanded. "Where is Merlin? Who attacks the castle?"

"Arthur is with his knights at The Table, preparing a final stand," she said.

The longer she tarried in the surrounding chaos, the more incomprehensible it became to her. Her wide eyes darted from here to there, perhaps looking for weakness. Or, maybe, she was just searching for a way out. Cassandra strode over to her and, without hesitation, kicked Morgana square in the jaw. I intervened and grabbed Cassandra by the shoulder. She shook me off and glared down at the sorceress.

"This is your doing, Morgana!" she yelled, contempt lacing her voice. "This is what you wanted. It's why you formed The Cabal. You've been playing with The Doorway to get Avery Black here!"

She grabbed a clump of Morgana's hair and pulled the woman's face upward to meet her gaze.

"What is your game here? Tell us now, or that kick will be as good as you get."

Another blaze of arrows streamed through the sky, followed by their flaming counterparts. In the spheres' fiery light, Morgana's watery eyes flashed as she regarded Cassandra. I suspected the Grecian prophetess looked quite different from their last interaction; weighted armor shaping her form rather than a flowing dress; her demeanor as sharp as the blade sheathed to her side.

"Quite the change in you, little prophet," Morgana remarked. "Black lift your curse? Does he believe the prattle from your ignorant mouth now? It's what you wanted all along – why you agreed to sit with the witches. Did he…" Her lips pulled into a wicked smile, "…make a woman out of you?"

I stepped forward to intervene, but Rowdy beat me to it. He pulled Cassandra away just as she prepared to deliver another kick, one that would undoubtedly disband Le Fay's head from her shoulders.

"She wants something you have, Avery," Cassandra said, wresting herself away from Rowdy's grip. "Or know – something that can change her course in history. In time."

I looked down on Morgana. She brazenly met my eye. We fought there a moment, the internal battle of wills waging stronger than the scathing one around us. Then, realization washed over me, seizing my bones with its chilled insight.

"You sent the dragon to Los Angeles," I whispered.

Morgana shook her head.

"He was already there. I simply engaged his services," she said with a sigh. "But he was too full of himself, as most dragons are, and didn't hold up his end of the bargain."

I dug deeper into my consciousness, desperately pulling away the pieces of this maddening puzzle to learn what she wanted. I was nearly there, the answer almost upon me, when another onslaught of arrows embedded their tips into my shield. I stumbled back against the force of it, my defensive barrier quivering just like my hands. A blazing bolder struck its bounds, and I was thrown forward by its power. Although precarious, my protection held. I landed on Le Fay, and the two of us folded together like lovers.

"We can still have her," she said in my ear. "Still win. You and I."

Cassandra approached my weakening shield.

"I have their leader. He is on the outer bluff."

Everyone followed her gaze. Through the haze of smoke and soot, the glint of golden armor was visible. Beside it, a man in robes pointed a staff at the battle before him as if directing its maneuvers.

"Mordred," Rowdy snarled. "And Merlin." Rowdy seemed confused. "But Merlin and Arthur are buddies. He gets the sword from The Lake and leads Camelot to a renaissance in which his people are content. So, what's this all about?"

"Look at the flags of the enemy," Cassandra stated. She gestured to their ranks then leveled her glower to Morgana. "Whose crest are they trumpeting?!"

"All is lost. All and forever," Morgana mumbled. Her grief-stricken gaze was held spellbound by the enchantment of her son's gilded armor. "Mordred has been taken from me. You were all I had left to save him."

"Your son?" Cassandra questioned, aghast. "Then, we need to end this now."

In two confident strides, Cassandra passed beyond my shield and drew a single arrow. Nocking it, she set her fingers upon the bowstring, then fortified her stance. She took in a single breath, gauging distance, wind, and a million other variables.

"It's an impossible shot," Rowdy said, more to himself than anyone else. "With a scope and a sniper rifle, I might not hit it."

Cassandra ignored the remark and raised the bow's curved frame. Its bronze tip glinted against the ashen sky. Around her, the noise was deafening. Yet, she was impervious to it, as she took in a breath and let the breath escape her lips. Then, she relaxed her grip and allowed the shaft to break from its strings.

She briefly watched its trajectory through the sky, seemingly confident that she had hit her mark.

"It's over, witch," she said, and turned to Morgana with an austere look.

"Is it?" Morgana rebuffed.

It took the arrow mere seconds to cut through the air over the battlefield before it hammered into Mordred's chest. Its force knocked him to the ground. In that instant, I felt the day could perhaps be won. Without its leader, an army can fracture and lose its focus.

Mordred's guard ran to his aide, but not Merlin. Instead, the old sorcerer searched from where the threat had arrived. He was looking for the bowman but leveled his eyes on me.

I squinted, adjusting my glasses the slightest bit.

"No. It cannot be," I said. "It's not Merlin at all."

Cassandra turned and looked on in shock as Mordred rose to his feet. His armor was untouched, and his rage-filled gaze found us from a distance. He drew his sword. Yet, Merlin stopped his advance and motioned to the castle gates.

Rowdy looked at Morgana.

"The magic armor?" he asked.

"No weapon of man my penetrate my spell upon it," she said pridefully.

Rowdy turned to me, bewildered.

"But that's from the movie *Excalibur*. Not from any history I've ever read. What the hell is going on here, Avery?"

A trumpet sounded. In the distance, Mordred mounted his horse and rallied his men. Merlin was nowhere to be seen.

Our time had finally run out.

"Rowdy, we need to find King Arthur! Now!" I ordered.

"I couldn't get a scent here if I tried. It's too much. Jo could but –"

"Go! Quickly!" I motioned to The Doorway that was still there behind us. "Mordred is heading to The Round Table. He must be stopped!"

Rowdy crossed to me. "This is a story, Av. A really realistic one, mind you, but still a –"

"It is *the* story," I interrupted. "I why we were brought here! One that countless writers, poets, and artists have drawn up for inspiration as a symbol of –"

"Hope," Rowdy said, understanding.

A barrage of arrows suddenly pierced through my sigil wall.

"Crap. Got it. Okay. Be back in a flash," Rowdy opened The Door, looked at Morgana Le Fay, then back to me. "Don't take your eyes off that one."

I nodded, and he and The Doorway were gone.

"Cassandra," I said, turning to her. "Get to the gates. Your training might be enough to rally the defenders."

Cassandra opened her mouth to protest. However, upon seeing the direness of the situation, she disappeared into the smokey haze without a word. I was alone with Morgana. I strode to her as she gained her feet.

"What have you done here?!" I demanded.

"She used me! Used all I had learned of you!" she said defiantly. "We were so close to immortality!"

Suddenly, the river to our backs began to churn. Its intensity was mounting with each passing moment. At the sight of it, Morgana instinctively backed away.

"No. No!" She looked at me, hysteria overcoming her. "I thought it was Merlin! I never wanted this. I swear. I told Merlin everything, thinking he had come to my side at last."

"It was never Merlin!" I countered.

As his name slipped from my tongue, the ravaging river ascended in height. Then, through the end foam, the Queen of

Avalon emerged. She was Lancelot's mother and the bearer of Excalibur, the sword that would rule England itself. She was held aloft by a pillar of water; its flow created her blue and white gown.

"It's Viviane!" I yelled at Morgana above the watery roar. "The Lady of The Lake!"

"Enough being part of history!" Viviane shouted. "Let us make some."

A thunder of river rose around her at her command. Then, she raised her hand and shoved her open-faced palm toward us. As the deluge crashed down, so did my shield.

ROWDY:
SHE WAS NOT THERE WHEN I OPENED THE DOOR.

THAT WAS NOT LIKE HER. JO COULD ALWAYS SEEM TO SENSE my arrival when The Doorway opened as if it created some kind of ripple her heightened senses alone could feel. I had grown to look forward to her jumping into my arms when I came to her. Now, the feeling was missed.

The Doorway dispersed me on the clifftops above the Colombia River. Beyond its waters, the sky was a brilliant blue, the air pungent with spruce and pine. I caught her scent in the wind, no panic or fear with it, and followed its unseen trail. I found Jo sitting cross-legged, looking down with her hands in her lap. Her back against a spruce tree that would one day be called The Cathedral Tree because it would live to be over three years old. Now, I guessed it was around eighty and just settling its roots.

"Pehnaho, Soleil Lune," she said.

Sun and Moon. She still had not looked at me, and her voice was far away.

I knelt beside her, and taking her hands, brought her to me. Slowly, she rested her head against my chest. She did not seem herself. It made me uneasy, like a teenager dreading being friend-zoned by his girl. Without Jo as my anchor, I would never survive this mad time trek from one harrowing E-ticket adventure to the next. How Avery did it, I would never understand. It must have been the hair.

"What is it?" I finally asked.

Jo moved away from me but did not answer. Instead, she lifted her gaze to the horizon. I followed it. Below us was the small city of Astoria, in what would one day become Oregon. It was just a village now in 1807, with a church and rows of houses and tents. An assortment of docks, where trappers unloaded their furs and fishing skiffs, painted the shoreline.

Although I did not have time to spare, we sat there a few silent moments, observing our surroundings. The first time Jo and I had visited Astoria was in 2021. Though it had grown from what we were looking at now, Jo told me that the oil on the river made it smell of sadness. So, we stuck to the 1807-ish version of the place.

"You need me," she said in Shoshone.

The use of her native language was done to make a point, for she and I spoke in English unless things were serious.

"That's why you are here," she concluded.

"Something wrong, babe?" I asked again.

"Do you tire of it?" she asked. "The struggle, I mean?"

And there is was – the point.

"It's what I am, Jo, what I do. It's how we met." I shrugged. "I wish that crappy, power-hungry people didn't come a dime a dozen. With the change in my pocket, I could probably buy a hundred."

It was not the first time this conversation had taken place, though this time felt more solemn – something had changed.

"Would you ever give it up?" she asked.

She did not need to add 'for me?'. As a guy who dances through time, one would be surprised by how quickly it runs out. But I was up against it, and we needed to go.

"Jo, I know you want to talk about this, but King Arthur is in a pickle, and Camelot is getting its ass handed to it."

Confused, and looked me in the eyes.

"But you told me it was a fairy table."

She was back to English, so things were looking up.

"I'm as puzzled as you are. Next, we'll be gluing Humpty Dumpty back together. But hey, we get to save The Round Table! Just be with me, Jo. Things have changed. Avery has Cass, and The Doorway seems like it's saying, 'the more, the merrier.'" I took her in my arms and did my best not to sound rushed. "You and I will be together. Come back to your people, your home…"

"Our home," she stated.

"Our home, whenever you want. Just be with me."

I could sense her happiness as she hugged me tighter. Then, she pulled away and gave me a curious gaze.

"So we go to save a table?" she asked.

"The Round Table!"

"So it's the shape that's significant?"

"Its shape is emblematic of all those sitting at it having an equal say in the…" I paused. "You're making fun of me, aren't you?"

She smiled. "It's very easy when you get on your box."

"My soapbox."

"Is it round, as well?"

"You can see for yourself," I replied.

I summoned The Doorway, but instead of going to it, Jo looked back at the children playing on the church grounds. She smiled at the sound of their laughter.

"Jo – honey, this is kind of important," I said.

She turned back to me.

"After saving the king, we will be together, Rowdy."

I nodded and led her to The Doorway. "After The King saving. Sounds good to me."

CASSANDRA:
WE MADE OUR STAND BACKED INTO CAMELOT'S
PORTCULLIS.

QUIVERS EMPTY. BODIES HAD BEEN PILED AT THE EDGE OF THE drawbridge, forcing the attackers to climb over the mound of the fallen. I fought with my swords, slicing through the openings of the chainmail and armor. The shadow of siege towers loomed over those who still held breath. Large, wheeled buildings, the battlements dropped ramps upon Camelot's walls. Then, the invaders breached and opened the gates from the inside.

On the opposite bank, the would-be king held his steed in check at the head of his cavalry. He was ready for the opening, fixed on trampling my lifeless body on his quest for power.

I motioned for him to come. He smiled, raised a hand high over his head, and let it fall. Somewhere behind him, unseen through the smoke of battle, a catapult let lose its deadly load. All of us on the bridge froze in shock as the flaming pitch-covered stone arced into the air. Men scrambled, throwing themselves from its lethal trajectory. Yet, there was nowhere to go.

As death reached its zenith high above me and began its flight back to earth, I stepped forward. My eyes were on the gold-clad daemon. I watched him lower his faceplate, a kind of metal mockery of the Japanese devil god masks. I crossed my two blades in front of my chest. *Ma-ki* and *Ti-mi* were slick with blood, showing my calm reflection on their silver surfaces. I would die with them in my hands. My Masters would be proud.

I did not close my eyes as the boulder fell towards me, blazing like the shell of the –

"Not today!" Rowdy yelled.

He grabbed me around the waist, his werewolf form throwing us from the drawbridge just as the world around us exploded.

The gate disintegrated. The defenders lay lifeless afore it. Then, even before the dust had cleared, the golden man drove his horse across the bridge.

At the last second, as Rowdy took me from the scene and toward the moat, I caught Mordred looking down at me from the smoking remnants of the bridge. If metal could laugh, I believed it did then. And it laughed at me.

.

AVERY:
THE WATER WAS UNRELENTING.

IT POUNDED DOWN ON ME – A TIDE WITHOUT A PAUSE between its crests. I kept backpedaling. My clothes were heavy, causing me to flop like a fish before the waves.

Viviane was akin to a god in this place, elevated by the river water that she rained down on me like a boxer who knew the fight was won.

I had to bide my time. Then, if the moment presented itself, I would snatch it up.

"Army of Avalon! You have laid too long beneath the waves!" Viviane's voice was a commanding echo across the conflict. "I have seen the future! My son will hold The Sword! Eternity beckons, and we will take its hand!" Then, she looked squarely down at me and smiled. "All thanks to you, Mr. Avery Black."

Morgana rose to her feet, her hands beginning to glow with an incantation. She thrust one of them forward, and a spear of red and yellow streaked towards our foe. But it was not to be. It glanced off Viviane's shoulder, the water there hissing.

Hissing. I tucked the thought away.

The Lady of the Lake laughed.

"The small-minded sorceress makes her last stand."

With a gesture, a ramrod of water slammed into Morgana like a freight train. I could hear ribs crack as one of the most powerful wizards in time, tumbled end over end across the blood-soaked grass. She came to rest, unmoving, mere feet from where I struggled to regain myself.

I shook the hair from my face. Water spread out in a fan around me.

"Never pictured you the villain, Viviane," I said, and backed away.

"Hero. Villain. It's all a matter of..." She clenched her fingers into a fist, and water gathered. "...perspective."

She slammed her watery fist down – a mistake. I evaded it and tumbled once more across the turf, farther from the river.

"Where is she, Black?"

The Lady Of The Lake advanced on me, the water crafting a blue-gray gown around her that slewed across the ground.

"Who?" I asked.

Talking was better than drowning, I thought.

"So, you are The Warlock Of History?" she surmised, unimpressed. "The one Cassandra discovered, and Le Fay hoped to harness along with your queen? I was expecting more."

"My queen?"

Viviane waved a hand, and water flew at me like bullets. The Cheyenne sign for ghost glowed on my skin, and they passed through me. Still, I felt them, which meant I was weaker than I believed.

She tilted her head to the side, studying me.

"Do you fancy yourself a…" she paused, deciding on the term, "…time-traveler? Morgana thought as much. Confided in me, as I wore the face of Merlin. He taught me how to shapeshift, did you know that?"

I nodded. "Yes. It's in the stories. Merlin was always fond of the ladies. Liked to impress. Not very decerning, though."

"There is no mention of you anywhere. I've looked. No witch or warlock notes your name. No religion. No prophet or scribe. Pythia. The oracle of Dione. Nothing."

I spat water from my mouth.

"Most find me a very private man,"

A gesture from her sent water flooding into me. I gagged the rapids, knowing that I did not have much time left.

"But I have done my own studying. With Merlin, using Morgana as my veiled disguise. Would you like to know what we found?"

The battle all but won she naturally had to expound on her greatness. Still, I could not help but wonder why villains are so incredibly verbose. Talk, talk, talk; it is all they do.

"You aren't a time traveler, little man." Viviane lifted me with a watery fist and slammed me to the earth. "You're a 'When' traveler. You don't travel through The Door at all."

Up again, down again. Then, Viviane raised me so that we were eye to eye and made the water I soaked turn to ice.

"The Door travels through you," she said. "And I really want that door."

ROWDY:
I PUT CASSANDRA DOWN NEXT TO THE CASTLE WALL.

It bordered the moat on one side where Jo waited beside the stone ramparts. Above us, the defense of Camelot was about to break. Mordred's army had breached the main gate, and the siege towers had dropped their ramps to storm the parapets.

"Find it?" I asked Jo. With her in human form and me in lychan, I loomed over her.

"Find what?" Cassandra said, somewhat irritated.

She had been prepared to die in battle, and here we were, all stealth-like yards away from its front lines. Evidently, it rubbed her the wrong way, making me miss the woman she had been before.

Jo pressed a single stone protruding from the wall. It made a clicking sound, and a hidden doorway opened to reveal a torch-lit passageway.

"The one named Arthur is through here," Jo said.

She seemed more irritated than Cassandra — if that was even possible.

Cassandra took the lead and passed into the gloomy corridor. Jo grabbed me by the arm and followed.

"This place is not real," she said. "The smells. The sounds. They are hollow and still. It's as if they were being conjured a moment before it appeared."

I smiled down at her. "I knew you'd find Arthur."

We made our way up the passage, stopping when Cassandra raised a forewarning. Jo drew her knife. I just waited, huffing, and puffing steam from my nostrils.

Voices came from a doorway ahead. Jo grabbed my nose, forcing me to hold my breath so we would not be heard. Cassandra drew a sword and, with her free hand, pushed her way into the room beyond.

King Arthur and half a dozen of his Knights Of The Round Table had been facing a far door, swords drawn, preparing to defend the table to the end. The ringing of swords resounded from the other side of the barred entry. The weight of the impending final defense of The Table and what it signified loomed within the chamber.

They turned as one to face Cassandra and Jo, forming a shield before Arthur. He held Excaliber, the sword's metal singing with power and cutting through the dark space with a brilliant glow.

"There he is, Rowdy," Jo said, cutting the silence. "Your King of Kings"

A pounding arose from the other side of the door. I knew it was Mordred and his guards attempting to eliminate the only obstacle left in their path to the crown. Arthur's knights seemed split by which threat to confront. They were outnumbered, crafting a hopeless situation.

Ugh. I owed Avery a quarter – never say 'hopeless.'

"Now what?" Cassandra asked.

She drew her other blade, and I stepped out of the shadows.

"We're here to save you," I said.

The knights that had decided to engage us a second ago took a visible step back, shocked by the fact that I was a ten-foot-tall werewolf.

"Sorcery," Sir Percival whispered.

"Wait. Look," I said.

I changed back into plain old Rowdy for them, hoping to lessen the tense atmosphere.

"I'm a human, just like you guys. I've even got a special sword like you."

I extended my right hand, and Shoshoni, my broadsword, appeared as if from thin air.

Cassandra eyed my blade.

"Where did you get that?"

"Ares gave it to me," I said.

"Ares *gave* it to you?" she repeated skeptically.

"Yeah. After he dropped it while I was kicking his ass."

"Rowdy, weapons from Olympus are not meant for mortal men to wield."

I tipped my wrist and gave it a little twirl. Then, I let go of it. Shoshoni levitated a moment, then came back into my hand.

"Oh, I'm sure you're right," I said with a hint of arrogance. "But I think you're just jealous because your swords can't talk."

Cassandra's eyes narrowed, and she started to argue, but I shook her off and approached Arthur.

"Look," I began. "I know this all seems pretty weird, but you need to trust me." I placed my hand on The Round Table for emphasis. "I have a way to save us."

The pounding on the other side of The Door was causing it to splinter. We were out of time. I drew the sword across my wrist, and blood spilled onto the tabletop.

"We'll need a chalice…or a grail."

AVERY:
VIVIANA HELD ME DOWN, SNEERING.

Her face was a watery, flowing mask. She studied my arms and the sigils on my skin.

"These symbols mark where you took The Doorway, Black. Imagine what the ones upon my skin will look like when I take my son Lancelot, with Avalon and Camelot's armies beneath a single banner, through the conquest of Everywhere and Everywhen."

With a flick of her wrist, she withdrew the water that had been pounding down on me, choking me.

"Where is she? Morgana might have been stupid enough to send an elder dragon to fetch her, underestimating its ability to divine what she was. But I am not that dim. I want your Queen of Time."

She turned her palm up, and the water plunged onto me, again, choking me. It was medieval waterboarding.

"I am the power in this world," she declared. "The sword I forged has led it, and once in the hands of Lancelot, it will bring about new world order. To every world, I will lead The Doorway."

Although muffled by the water pouring into my ears, the sound of her voice sounded strong, as if she felt victory in her grasp.

"I will drown you and bring you back until I have what I want, Doorwayman. I need the girl. History's keeper. Need to whisper in her ear and forge reality to me."

"If you want Eve," I yelled. "You will need more water."

I reached out to Rowdy through my mind and told him that it was now or never.

ROWDY:
KING ARTHUR SAT AT THE HEAD OF THE ROUND TABLE.

LANCELOT, GAWAIN, PERCIVAL, KAY, AND PERCIVAL WERE THE only knights that remained.

The bar across the door cracked, and Mordred rushed in with his guard. His unscratched armor gleamed, and I knew that without Le Fay's enchantment, he would have never made this far. Then he lifted his faceguard and observed the room before turning his attention to the King. Excalibur lay on the table between them.

"Uncle," he said.

"Nephew." Arthur curled his lip in disgust. "Traitor."

"It is for the greatness of Camelot I do this."

"Killing those protecting this castle. Those brave knights who sat at The Round Table. This is how you measure greatness, Mordred?" Arthur rebuffed. "Lay down your sword, and I will make your death a quick one."

Mordred laughed, drawing his blade. "Funny. I was about to say the same to…"

Mordred's declaration fell mute when a low growl rumbled out from the darkness behind the king. Each snarl that

followed grew louder and louder. I had given the knights a drop of my lycan blood. The transformation might have lasted only a minute or two, not as long as the curse of a bite, but I was hoping that would be all we needed to turn the tide. Then, a silver chalice flew out from the blackness, landing on The Round Table. The remainder of the lycan blood splashed from its basin and across the wooded tabletop.

"My mother has found a doorway," Mordred said.

Uncertainty coated his voice. Clearly, he was skeptical of what was taking place, thinking victory had been his.

The din behind King Arthur intensified, gnashing of fangs and scratching of long talons on the stone floor. I told them to do that. It added to the drama.

Mordred's men looked close to panic, stepping back.

"A…doorway," Mordred stammered. "…through which Camelot can spread its influence across all time."

"With you in my seat, I assume?" Arthur added flatly.

He stood and took Excalibur in hand, testing its weight and finding it true. Then, he looked to the would-be king, eyes level and tone one of authority.

"For Camelot!" he declared.

The drop of my blood changed him as it had his knights into lycans. They charged forward, a howling horde of beasts that descended on Mordred's guard.

I chose to stay human and guarded Arthur's back, fighting alongside the king with my broadsword. King Arthur slashed at Mordred and met his blade with Excalibur. Mordred's golden armor, which once could not be pierced by weapons of man, was getting torn to shreds with each strike of Arthur's talons. All too quickly, Mordred retreated, his blade fending off the lethal blows as he struggled for his bearings.

The situation seemed grave, but I was having the time of my life. I sliced candles in half, kicked chairs into my opponents, and pulled adorning tapestries down on their heads. Had there been a chandelier there, I would have swung from it. All the while, Shoshoni hummed and as she met every blade that came at me. Once, I bumped into Lancelot and gave him a withering glare.

"You're foster mother, Viviane, is making a real mess of it out there, pal!"

"Any whom attack Arthur and Camelot attack me, as well," Lancelot replied. "Be it the woman who raised me or not."

He looked and sounded every part of the hero, so I took him at his word and kept on fighting.

Cassandra whirled and ducked through the melee, seemingly everywhere at once. Jo staved off any attempt by Mordred's men to escape through the entrance we had used. Then, I saw Mordred seize a fatal opportunity when Arthur stumbled. He raised his blade to strike at Arthur's neck. Yet, he never got the chance. I threw Shoshoni like a spear and hit Mordred square in the helmet, snapping back his head and throwing off his sword arm.

Arthur, the once and future king, plunged his taloned fist through his nephew's chest. Mordred slumped and slid to the floor, dead, his quest for glory dying with him. His men ran from the fight in wholesale retreat.

We all stood there a long moment, panting, taking it all in. I locked eyes with Cassandra, who smiled at me from across the room. Then, I went to Jo and hugged her. All the knights lifted their heads as one and roared in a werewolf victory howl that resounded throughout Camelot and across the battlefield, alerting everyone who heard of how *I* saved the day.

AVERY:
VIVIANE FALTERED AT THE TRUMPET-LIKE SOUND OF
HOWLING FROM WITHIN THE CASTLE.

MY CREW TO THE RESCUE! IT WAS NO OR NEVER.

I called on the fiery symbol of Atar and brought it to my hand. I had marshaled my strength, given to me by countless cultures in my journeys by the sigils that told their stories.

The sigil's power glowed, and the water that held me down was transformed into steam. The sudden change caused The Lady Of The Lake to recoil in pain and confusion. Suddenly free, I got to my feet and ran from her as far and as fast as I could. She pursued me as I had hoped.

In the distance, a riderless white horse stood upon the field of battle, its red and green bridle hanging across its neck. I went to it and gave its forehead a calming pat.

"Be brave for me," I said.

Then, I righted his bridle and swung myself up into the saddle. My free hand showed it the symbols of the wolf, bear, and eagle. The horse received my meaning, and lifting its head with newfound purpose, reared in a show of strength and defiance. It blew air through its nostrils with such force that it.

sounded like a roar and that I knew I had chosen well. Then, I picked up the reins, and together, we rode out to face our foe.

I could see Viviane as she watched in shock as her forces fell back from Camelot's walls. Above the battlements, King Arthur rallied his followers. I grabbed one of his battle flags that had been staked in the turf and raised it in the air as I rode. It caught The Lady Of The Lake's attention, and I squared off for our final confrontation.

"We could have made history together," she said to me.

"Been there. Done that," I retorted.

I kicked the horse to a gallop. Viviane placed her hands before her and summoned the river. Only then did she see how far she had gone from the water's edge. I saw her mortified expression as she realized that all of my falling back had not just been for show.

She hurriedly retreated to the river. The water around her leaped to her defense, forming a pond and liquid walls in her wake. With all of my remaining strength, I called upon the symbol of Prometheus, letting its lightning course through the flag's shaft until it ignited into yellow and blue flames. Then, I tucked it under my arm like a jousting lance and charged.

Viviane turned to face me in that last instant before impact. As she raised her hands in defense, blood from the battle she had lost dripped from her fingertips. My white horse reared at the aquatic boundaries that encased her. In that same moment, I drew back the flaming standard and forcefully drove it into her chest. Her scream cut through the air, and the world around me exploded into vapors. Then it dispersed into nothing more than the whistle from a teapot.

Camelot had held.

I AM AVERY BLACK. I never know where or when my door will open. But once the knob begins to turn, I and those with me will answer the summons, cross the threshold, and greet what lies beyond.

THE WORLDS OF AVERY BLACK

A GLOSSARY OF CHARACTERS AND TERMS

Pleased To Meet You

AVERY BLACK:
Known by many names, from The Eternal Man to Doorwayman, Avery is mankind's avatar of Hope. A traveler through a slipstream of eternity, the sigils covering his body speak of humanity's journey since its inception. They are thousands of fluctuating, living tattoos that enable him to manifest their power at will and bring hope he encounters beyond The Doorway.

CASSANDRA: A Trojan priestess and the daughter of the King of Troy, her beauty found the eye of the Greek god Apollo. He granted her the gift of prophecy, but after spurning his affection, he cursed her never to be believed. She is now the face of The Witches Cabal; the embodiment of all spellcasters and sorceresses are waiting within her.

THE DOORWAY: A portal to everywhere and everywhen. Though Avery's name is on the frosted glass, its origins and intents are unknown. When it knocks, Avery has always answered.

LYCHAN and WEREWOLF: Sons of King Lychan, cursed by Zeus to take the form of a wolf, are different in many ways from their cursed brethren, the werewolf. Humans cursed to be a werewolf change on the full moon, losing their humanity during that cycle. However, King Lychan's direct sons can transform into werewolves at any time and still retain their human intelligence. They are strongest upon the rising of the full moon.

ROWDY CROWE: America's first werewolf, 250 years old. He is the only known mix of lychan and werewolf blood, wielding incredible strength, speed, and near-instant healing capabilities, while still holding onto his humanity. Having lived so long, it has also given him an off-kilter sense of humor and a seldom seen, but just as useful, understanding of his job traveling alongside Avery.

SACAJAWEA: A Shoshone Indian whose tracking skills helped the famous explorers Lewis and Clark during their expedition in the Louisiana Territories. Many believed she died in 1812, but in fact, she was bitten by a werewolf, fled her family, and was later rescued by Rowdy.

SIGILS AND SIGNS: From early caveman drawings to present-day street signs, hieroglyphics to spray-painted graffiti, the sigil, or sigilla, are signs of humankind's culture and contain incredible strength and knowledge. The holder of these sigils can manifest ancient energy, tapping into the core of the very universe itself.

EVE: The embodiment of The Tree Of Knowledge. Walking through time, drawing in all that is known. Always awake. When consciousness is lost, knowledge can be manipulated by whomever whispers in her ear.

THE ELDER: Thousands of years old, an ancient of unspeakable being of guile and power. Whatever form it choses, its desire is power and wealth. Then more power and more wealth.

JOE and VIC: Trackers and warriors, Rowdy can call upon when needed. Time will show how much more they really are.

THE SWORD NUTHUNG: Wielded by Sigurd in Norse mythology, it slayed the great power-hungry dragon Fafnir, who guarded a golden hoard.

LOS ANGELES: An ethnically diverse city of over 18.7 million souls, the area drawing history and power from its beginnings when claimed by Spain in 1542. Conquering Los Angeles would be a good stepping-stone to conquering

Werewolves of London

BABA YAGA: A Slavic witch with tremendous supernatural powers. She can be asked for help, and it is in the nature of the request and the person who is asking, which often ties her to the actions she must follow.

THE CABAL OF WITCHES: Cloaked in darkness and led by a supreme and anonymous woman, the cabal is made of witches throughout time. Cassandra is their personification in the modern world.

DAMARCHUS HILL: An ancient, powerful werewolf from Avery's past. A true emissary of Anger, he uses his staff to help channel his emotions into a powerful force for evil.

HAROLD LLOYD: An early 20th-century American actor, comedian, and stunt performer. He appeared in many silent films but is best known for dangling from the minute hand on a giant skyscraper clock face in Los Angeles in 1923.

JACK THE RIPPER: A serial killer who was never apprehended. Though the police in late 19th century London had many suspects, the Ripper murders were never solved, and the killings ended mysteriously.

STONEHENGE: A prehistoric monument thousands of years old that still stands today in Wiltshire, England. It is made up of huge sarsen stones that rest above a burial site.

Opinions differ about what the actual patterns of the stones were used for and who put them there.

VICTORIAN LONDON: In 1888, the industrial city was overcrowded and rife with pollution and crime, making it a miserable place to live for the working class. It did have a huge clock called Big Ben that could be heard throughout the city and still stands today.

QUOTES, PEOPLE, PLACES, AND FACTS: Inside the Avery Black World, Time plays an important part and is a character in the stories (The Doorway). Because of this, a variety of famous people, places, and movies are referenced. So, drink it in. Look up Thermopylae. Or Benny Goodman. Or who lived on Baker Street. You never know what's out there. You just might find something cool.

TURNING JAPANESE

AVERY'S GLASSES: Why won't those things come off? Are they just normal glasses? Well, in answer to that, only he can take them off, and no, they aren't anything close to normal. But I can't give everything away in the first book, right?

BUSHI: The word for 'warrior' in the Japanese language is often used to refer to a Samurai. The origin of Bushi dates to the year 743.

GASHADOKURO: A giant skeleton made from the bones of the dead who did not have a proper burial. The only way to stop the giant monster is to make it angry.

HAJIMEYOU: "Let's begin."

NINJA: Like Samurai and Bushi that are unique to Japan, Ninjas are trained assassins. Skilled in special combat techniques referred to as 'Ninjutsu', they are living weapons, period. Or, actually, exclamation point. You didn't think I would make it easy on Rowdy, did you?

THE NINTH LEGION: Legio IX Hispana was one of the most decorated and successful of Roman Legions. They fought in Caesar's campaigns from Spain to Scotland. However, they disappeared around 120 A.D. Many historians and authors have tried to explain what happened. I figured I would give it a go.

OKIUNION CEMETERY: A beautiful ancient cemetery in Japan. During visiting hours, it is serene and spiritual. However, stories abound of spirits that haunt the place after dark, chanting and moaning. It's a good place for a ghost fight, especially at 2:30 a.m.

ON BEING 256 YEARS: Why is Rowdy that old? What was happening in America 256 years ago in 1765? Good question. I thought, with Rowdy being such a revolutionary character, a mix of lychan and werewolf, he should begin his journey in a revolutionary year.

ONI: An ogre-like demon guardian, it carries a club called a 'kanabo', which it uses with deadly force to protect its master. I wasn't going to make it easy on Cassandra, either.

PIZZA MARGHERITA: There are a lot of stories of how and when pizza started being pizza. I liked the one that included the chef's name, Raffaele Esposito, who supposedly made it to honor the Margherita of Savoy.

SAMURAI: Meaning 'warrior' or 'knight' in Japanese, this class of soldier was held to a code of honor. Relentless training in many different fighting styles and weaponry were paramount in achieving this class distinction. What Cassandra went through was tough – like that, times ten.

SOUTHWICK HOUSE: If you are going to start a fight, start it where the biggest one of all time started. D - Day, June 6th, 1944, began here.

YUREI: Ghosts barred from a peaceful afterlife; Japanese folklore describes them as very vengeful because they still hold onto the suffering of their mortal existence. Yurei's tend to wear white, have black hair, and have been disfigured. They ask their would-be male prey about their beauty before attacking; 2:30 a.m. is their witching hour.

Olympus – Winner Takes It All

APOLLO: In Greek mythology, he is the god that pulled the sun across the sky with his chariot to create dawn and dusk. He is infinitely handsome and great at everything from music to fighting. In all, he is a god's god. Unfortunately, he has the ego to match. He is not a good loser because he seldom loses; he thinks he has the goods on everybody who comes against him.

ARES: The god of war, he represents the slaughter and brutality of combat. However, he is Zeus' son, so he gets a lot of slack for all the bloodshed. He has, however, taken his share of beat downs and can scamper off to fight another day if everything is not going his way.

CASSANDRA AND APOLLO: Cassandra has the gift of prophecy, but when she spurns Apollo and his advances (see above about him and losing), she is cursed to be a liar to all, no matter what she says, true or not, she is not believed. A girl might do anything, go through anything, to have a curse like that be lifted.

GREEK GODS: They live on Mount Olympus with the All-Father Zeus. They look down on Earth and come up with all sorts of things for mortals to do, from vanquishing to honoring and so on. They are ancient but powerful. To this day, thousands of people still visit the ruins of their temples and shrines.

PANDORA AND HER BOX: Pandora cannot help but look into the box gifted to her by Zeus. Although she is told not to open it, she releases all the physical and emotional demons that mankind suffers from today when she does lift the lid. Once she slams it closed, the only thing remaining that humanity can hold against all the misery she let loose is Hope. So, I took that story and thought, "Hmmmm…we can do something with that."

End of the World As We Know It

ASTORIA, OREGON: Located near the mouth of the Columbia River, it was the first American settlement west of the Rocky Mountains. It has a history with the Lewis and Clark Expedition because that is where the explorers established a winter camp at Fort Clatsop.

CAMELOT: The castle and court of the legendary King Arthur and the Knights of the Round Table. Symbolic of Arthur Pendragon's realm of might for right in opposition to war and greed for power, it is not just a mythical castle in Britain. It is a legendary icon that has inspired countless authors, poets, and songwriters throughout the centuries. For a funny take, go with the Monty Python version. Like a good musical? You might enjoy Lerner and Loewe's *Camelot*. Movies? *Excalibur. First Knight* – Richard Gere's Philadelphia accent is well worth the watch. In the book world, there's Mark Twain's, *A Connecticut Yankee in King Arthur's Court*. If you're into a more serious literary route, have a go at T. H. White's epic novel, *The Once and Future King* or the 15th-century prose of Thomas Malory's *Le Morte d'Arthur*. Just so many versions to enjoy.

THE LADY OF THE LAKE: Viviane, Queen of Avalon, gave Arthur the sword, Excalibur, and she raised Lancelot, who was the best of Arthur's knights. She was also an enchantress trained by the sorcerer Merlin.

EXCALIBUR: The legendary sword given to King Arthur by the Lady of the Lake. It was attributed magical powers that can only be used by the rightful sovereign of Britain.

MERLIN: King Arthur's friend and advisor, one of the most powerful wizards in literary history. He was a master of disguise and shapeshifting. According to legend, he taught the art Viviane and Morgana.

MORDRED: The son of Morgana Le Fay and traitorous nephew of King Arthur intent on usurping the throne of Camelot.

MORGANA LE FAY: Sorceress. Enchantress. She was always scheming to get the best for her son, Mordred, who is also always scheming to get the best for himself. No matter what version of this myth you follow, mother and son tend to come up short.

THE ROUND TABLE: Not the square or rectangular one. It's the table where King Arthur and his knights convened and would all have an equal say in the just ruling of the realm.

Since it was round, it symbolized that no one was sat at the head of the table. Therefore, no one in attendance had more power than the other.

END NOTES:
By now, it is obvious that the title of this book and each work within it was named after either song title or a song verse. Here's the list:
Time After Time: A song by Cyndi Lauper (1983)
Pleased to Meet You: A line from the Rolling Stones song, *Sympathy for the Devil* (1968)
Werewolves of London: A song by Warren Zevon (1978)
Turning Japanese: A song by The Vapors (1980)
Winner Takes It All: A song by ABBA (1980)
It's The End Of The World As We Know It: (And I Feel Fine.) A song by R.E.M. (1987)

CHARACTER SONGS: A long time ago, in a writing class in college, I was told to put a song with a character to keep in your mind when writing them. So, I thought I would share my three lead character tunes with you here:
AVERY: *Time After Time* by Cyndi Lauper
ROWDY: *No One Lives Forever* by Oingo Boingo
CASSANDRA: *She's Always a Woman to Me* by Billy Joel

ABOUT THE AUTHOR

Christopher Harvill created Avery Black over 35 years ago in Alhambra, CA, so if the main character has a bit of that 1980's INXS hair going for him, blame that. He is a screenwriter, children's book author, and comic book artist. He also feeds horses on his ranch and tries to be as good a husband, father, and as creative a writer as he can be.

Made in the USA
Monee, IL
31 December 2021

391adc9a-c674-4b15-9f66-b9398397bb2aR01